S0-BZS-092

"In Rabindranath Tagore's footsteps, Richard Payment writes beautifully, and generates a moving evanescence, working, as he does, in the age-old but always compelling area between writing and dreaming. This is as much a prose poem as it is a novel, the kind of book and writer we must not lose in the new unsatisfying welter that corporate book publishing has become."

FRANK DELANEY
author, journalist and broadcaster

"A fresh voice, one that follows its own promptings and isn't going to be marshalled by what other people might want. It's about discovery, very much in tune with the zeitgeist."

ELIZABETH BUCHAN
author of *Light of the Moon*, *I Can't Begin to Tell You*, *Revenge of the Middle Aged Woman* and other novels

"The book is a true gift and guide to better understand the quest for and sources of euphoria and completeness."

AMY BARONE
poet, author of *Kamikaze Dance*

"I adore the sparse style and the easy melody of the prose. A natural writer, this fellow. The narrator, Vishesh Darshane, is endearing and I would follow him to the ends of the Earth."

SONJA YOERG
author of *House Broken*, *Middle of Somewhere* and *Clever as a Fox*

The world will never starve for want of wonders,
but only for want of wonder.

G.K. Chesterton

FOR WANT OF
WONDERS

RICHARD PAYMENT

Published by daisyamerica LLC

Cover photograph: © James Gallagher

First hardcover edition: 2015

ISBN 978-1-932406-03-4

10 9 8 7 6 5 4 3 2 1

Printed in the United States of America
by King Printing Co., Inc.
181 Industrial Avenue, Lowell MA USA 01852
www.kingprinting.com

The traveller has to knock
at every alien door to come to his own,
and he has to wander through all the outer worlds
to reach the innermost shrine at the end.

Rabindranath Tagore

The world is full of magic things,
patiently waiting for our senses to grow sharper.

W.B. Yeats

1

I have a story to tell

*Faith is the bird that feels the light
when the dawn is still dark.*

Rabindranath Tagore

REMEMBERING

I am remembering something.

At first it comes to me as a feeling. It is comforting. It is a place I want to be. It is home.

Is it the memory of a dream? It is indistinct, but real. I am holding only a thread. And I do not want to let go.

Maybe it is a movie I saw, a book I once read or a piece of conversation, the clarity of an idea that is so simple that it is beauty. It is the comfort I want, the protection that embraces.

Then it comes back all at once: a woman on a beach, a tree, a wind that calms, a rain that cleanses, but does not wet.

My memories are nothing but looped reruns I cannot change. But this one memory is different. There is no regret, no disappointment. I do not want to adjust it, fix the focus or rewrite the script. I return to its shores because this one memory is my comfort. It is not the past. It is not the future. It is my home beyond my home. It will always be the present.

Stop me if you have heard this all before. It might sound familiar. It might have happened to you.

Remember this: my name. It is Vishesh. Vishesh Darshane. Can you remember that? You can call me Vishesh or Vijay, Raj or even Jimmy if you wish, if it is easier. I have been many things, but none had to do with my name. And, if I am to admit the truth, none of them had anything to do with me as a person.

Be still. Remember my name. It is the label that is attached to me. It is the one thread that is sewn through this entire story. Your story or my story – it is only the stitching that changes. The want is the thing that drives us.

Trust me: I have a story to tell.

ONE MEMORY

I was ten. It was May, the hottest of months. I was on the beach in my hometown, Nargol, in southern Gujarat, on the west coast of India. I had been playing cricket with other boys. I remember because my legs were tired and I was happy. I was satisfied.

When I say "playing," that might be an exaggeration. My legs were not tired from running, jumping for the ball, exertion of any kind. My legs were tired from simply standing. If sitting squat, cross-legged on the ground had been an option, a cricket approved position, that would have been my choice – in the middle of the action, but not part of it.

The truth is I loved being a part of the game. I enjoyed it very much. I did not enjoy the playing. There is a difference. Being a part is acceptance. Playing is dangerous. Both injury and humiliation are the risks. I was usually in the distant outfield, in the area least likely for the ball to travel. That is where they wanted me. And that is where I wanted to be.

I delighted in cheering on the others, keeping score on a scrap of paper or in the dirt with a stick or the heel of my shoe. I was a cheerleader, a support, but what I liked most was the numbers. Sometimes, when the game was slow or I was bored, I would siphon a handful of the sandy dirt between my fingers. Like a potion of magic, if I could count every last grain before they slipped through, returning to the ground, I would understand. The count was the knowledge.

"Mother Earth," I thought, "if the ball rolls this way, use all your grains to stop it. You are so many. The ball is only one." It was a prayer more than a thought.

I knew even then that, like those grains, I was one among millions. There were five million or more other boys my age in India, every one of them as cricket-mad as the next. In height, in schoolwork, in talent, in every way, it seemed, I did not stand out. Yet when I was alone with myself, I knew there was more – more than just getting ahead, more than standing out in the crowd, catching the ball or winning a match.

Perhaps those were my thoughts on that day. My luminous memory, singular and pure, is this: the game is ending, the boys are tired but not dispersed, the ball is still occasionally rising high through the air, but the desire to run, to catch is gone.

I see a woman in a white sari and a red shawl. At first, it is the colour that catches my eye, then it is her grace and movement. She is at the shoreline, the very edge where water and land meet. There is a give and take, a partnership between the two.

I follow her. At a distance. Compelled. The shouts and voices of the game recede, erased by the waves, the continuous roll of water. My distance from her is respectful.

She turns from the shore, towards a grove of small trees, bushes and stubbled grasses. She sits under one tree, much like the others, windbent and weathered. She closes her eyes. It seems like meditation, not sleep. It is silence. Deep.

My attention is sharp and focused. I am closer than the actual distance between us.

She is beauty. And she is peace. She reminds me of no one. Do I know her? Is she from Nepal? Is she Gujarati? Her age is beyond determination. I cannot count. My math does not work. The moment is complete to itself. It is both new and familiar. It is real and vibrant. There is a gentle power and a perfection.

Then it came. Out of a clear sky, a rain, torrential. Not water so much as light and energy – vibration. She does not move. Shelter is not needed.

If you have this feeling as I did, you might also never forget. It was magnificent and grand. If you had this experience, you might want to run and tell the world. But after the running, the words fail. Language is limited. But my awareness did not fail. My awareness, my attitude and understanding did not change. They opened. Like a door. Like a curtain. Like a current of electricity that reaches a bulb. The filament glows in the glassed vacuum. It glows bright. And then, all at once, it fills the darkened room with light, a rich and bathing luminance.

She sat there for some time. I also sat. For how long, I am unsure. Meditation does not know the hand of the clock.

I am no longer that boy. But still, inside, I am that boy unchanged. I am Indian, but I hope I am also something more – of the world and beyond the world. But for all my aspirations, I still stand, a ten year old boy on that shore, in that moment, a complete witness.

There is a direct line between that moment and now. It is undiminished by time. How does that rain falling in Nargol differ from the rain falling now on my metal-framed, double-glazed city window? It is different in every way.

CRICKET

Sometimes you can love a thing and not even know you love it. It can be so much a part of your life that you just figure everyone loves it as much as you. Your love is nothing special. It is a love that you feel is obvious. It is nothing to hide, natural.

So it was with me and cricket. Oh, I loved that game: cricket this, cricket that. But I didn't know until years later to call this feeling love.

My love was a true love, but the love of an outsider watching. The watching was everything. There was never a thrill in holding the bat. I just wasn't that good. Chasing a ball was even worse. Bounding and bouncing across the field, what was I to do? It might as well have been a rabbit or a monkey or a diseased rat eager to puncture my skin with its rabid teeth. That is how much I wanted to touch the thing. Picking it up before it crossed the boundary line would mean having to throw it. Throwing it would mean having to have both speed and accuracy at the same time. Not having those talents would mean ridicule.

Standing in the outfield at the ready was close enough for me – too close if the action ever came my way. My love for cricket came from afar. The love was my companion, not the game.

I know now, my real thrill for the game was in the score-keeping – the numbers, the rankings, the averages and, most importantly, the odds. What if this bowler was paired against that batsman? What if my beloved team won at least two of the next four games, what would be the odds of advancing? It wasn't the competition. It was the calculation. It wasn't the sharp sound of bat on ball. It was the sound of the sharpening of my pencil.

In my mind, the woman on the beach and playing of cricket were always connected. For a long time, I could not think about one without remembering the other. Really, it's not that the two were all that similar. There was some other quality that was more vital and direct, and also at the same time, beautiful and delicate, a thread connecting the two. It went beyond the fact that both took place near the Nargol shore or that one lead seamlessly into the other.

As I look back, I can see that both events held an element of witnessing. I was not a participant in either. I stood back, not passive, but certainly detached. I was playing, but not playing. I was there, but not there. But beyond that, there was another feeling. Inside, a vibrant awareness held me. It reached out with an aura of protection. I realize now that that feeling was something quite simple and also quite real. It was as real as the wind – something that cannot be seen.

As I watched the cricket matches, I felt myself to be in a world that I could control. Cricket was a game I could comprehend, a realm of rules and moves and, above all, friends – a place that I understood, but which also understood and accepted me.

When I saw the woman on the beach, I was also enveloped, sheathed and swathed in that same cloak of understanding. To put it simply: what I felt was love.

But while the love of cricket was a passion, switched on and off with each win or loss, the woman on the beach exuded something more. Hers was a love of a higher level, without condition, pure, unending.

On the cricket field, I was an outsider, but my heart lead me. I trusted its lead. Let those others boys sweat, tear their precious trousers, bloody their knees and noses. I knew the percentages, the angles, the odds. I also knew pure love.

Put it this way: cricket made me feel happy, that woman made me feel joy.

MATCH

It was a day like many others, a cricket day. I stood my ground on the beach side of the field, the sea to my back. I liked that position. The sea breeze kept me cool. It also limited the drive of the ball, keeping it in, shortening its range. It was a fair advantage, a compensation for my lack of athletic might.

To my right and left, the other fielders had sided in closer to me, guarding the gap created by my slow responses and even slower running.

I loved the perfection of the game. Sometimes I even loved being in the game in a certain way: on the field, part of the mechanics, the clockwork dictated by the movement of the ball, boys moving with precision, this way, that way, dodging with all their attention.

The thing I didn't like was the spotlight the ball brought with it, when all the attention fell on me.

Words can tell a story, numbers a different story. Let me continue. I was thinking about many things at once – nothing and everything – school, not being in school, school tomorrow. I was thinking of a seagull, the way it can hold itself steady in the air like a kite pushed by the wind, but also pushing against the wind, a small movement of the wing, a slight correction and there, its position recovered, the balance maintained. Does a bird play or is it a part of the play? What would it be like to be a bird looking down on a cricket field, seeing a ball rise and grow, white like an egg, spinning?

"Whoa, whoa, whoa!" The ball was not rising. It was falling. Towards me, growing. Directly. I raised my arms to shield my face. I reached to grasp and to defend at the same time. Squarely, solidly, like a magnet, the cricket ball met the palm of my hand. My fingers responded, grasped it tightly. There was no thinking.

Numbers tell one story: one ball, one catch, one victory. The count was in and recorded: statistically insignificant, ninety-nine failures versus one lucky catch.

Words tell another story: a long season of fumbles and errors erased by one victorious catch. Jai!

There was a thunder. "Vi-vi-vi-shesh." They called my name for all that it was worth – everything. It wasn't just a catch. It was the complete match. My natural defense, a reaction without thought or plan, had saved the day. Victory was ours. And I was included.

Elevated, my pay-off really came in the next match. In choosing sides, I was no longer the last pick.

Even the gull, still hanging in the sky, was enjoying.

SCHOOL

Sometimes I can see things that others cannot. I am not talking about a dead uncle at the dinner table or a spectre shimmering in a poorly lit mirror. Those are things I wouldn't want to see. I am not talking about UFOs or an angel wrapped in the kitchen curtains watching, waiting to intervene before tragedy strikes. I am just talking about detail. People don't see it. I don't know what they are looking at, but it is not the obvious. They see the pattern, the outline, the impression, but they do not see what goes into making that pattern.

"Draw a picture of the animal you would like to be." This is one of my earliest memories. The classroom is quickly filling with images of elephants and lions and loyal dogs, kings of the jungles, the fierce, the fantastic. Is a dragon allowed? I can draw an elephant with my eyes closed. Lions also: eyes, whiskers and a fury of mane – there's your lion, sir.

I don't know where it came from. What I really wanted was to be a nightingale. There are no nightingales in India. Maybe I just liked the name or the idea – not a hawk, nor an eagle, a falcon or vulture, flying the highest, with slow effortless circles, able to see and to scare. These birds are show-offs. Like the star bowlers at the all-day cricket tournaments, they were too obvious, too visible. I wanted to be stealth. I wanted to be a nightingale. I read it somewhere. Or more likely someone read it to me. Tales from Shakespeare perhaps. Probably.

The sky is still dark, but it is morning. The nightingale sings to wake the other birds. Change is coming. Wake up. Don't miss it. Hey, Hawk, still tired from all your high flying? It's a new day. Hear my song. This day is like no other. Are you going to miss it, flying so high? Can't you see past your own beak?

My pencil scribbles violently. I am drawing the darkness, all the blackness. It will end. Listen to my song. With the bird invisible in the black, how was I to draw a voice, a single call? I can hear it. The lazy lions and stupid elephants were still sleeping, drugged, overdosing, ignorant.

We were not Christian and certainly not Catholic. It was just an opportunity and my parents took it. The missionary school on Ashoka Road, exactly one mile from our house, offered free schooling to good Catholic boys. It offered a desk, an endless supply of pencils and a school uniform with a snappy maroon necktie to Christians boys of any hue, any degree of commitment. It was a missionary school. Their mission was to get me to heaven. But for opportunists like me, it offered a bonus: a hand-cranked pencil sharpener fixed to the bookshelf next to the window. Choose your pencil size, crank for as long as you want, take in the view. The world was there to see – or at least the cricket field that adjoined the school. That was world enough. The sea was somewhere beyond.

It wasn't exactly a complete education, but it was a schooling – enough to get you going. Change your name to Michael or Joseph and, lo, you are a Catholic – and a Roman in the same deal. At home I was Vishesh. At school I was Thomas. In my own world I was a centurion and secretly a nightingale, a double agent, stealth, invisible, known by an array of names – Superfly, Hanuman, Agent V and nameless-for-now – able to see what others cannot.

After school, I was invisible in the darkness at the cowdust time – Godhuli Bela. My mother would call me to the safety of our home.

"Be inside now, the night is coming. Lord Krishna is bringing his cows to safety." I wanted to be with the nightingales ready for the morning sun, but I also wanted to be with my mother. "Now is the time when the Earth does yoga," she said. I looked down the distant road. I could see the dust in the red light.

Krishna's cows moved too slowly.

MOTHER

My mother was a saint.

They told us about the saints in school. A dour and sour crowd. I cannot imagine those saints playing cricket, laughing, enjoying this world. They were martyrs mostly – grim, determined only to go to heaven after a life of penance, no time to fly a kite.

My mother was not that kind of saint. Still, I don't remember ever seeing her read a book or going to a movie. Her life was her children – all five of us. She told us stories – not from books, but from her memory, not only for our entertainment, but for our betterment.

I know that if I could travel back now and stand watching my mother in the kitchen of our house, I might think, "There is a woman of an older fashion, a woman from another age, walking seven steps behind her husband, carrying on her life in a cycle of chores – shopping, cleaning, cooking, serving a family who would then go on to serve the world." My mother was a woman beyond fashion, old or new. This is something that can be seen now. I could not see it when I was in her kitchen.

The past is a faraway place from which we have been exiled with no hope of return. With no court of appeal, no lawyer to argue our case, we cannot go back. Our visa has been revoked. We can no longer participate, yet we dwell on it, hoping there will be an invitation.

My mother does not know of all the things that have happened to me after I left India, just as I do not know of all the things she did before I was born. Our lives overlap so briefly.

Children believe in the eternal.

My mother called to me, "Come in Vishesh. Your food is waiting."

I thought she would always be there to beckon me, to feed me, to prepare my way and pick up after me. Children do not know real change. They believe the present will go on forever.

"Why do you not hear me? Your brothers are eating now."

I remember my mother. She is crouching next to me. We are at the side of the road. I am wrapping a string around a stick tighter and tighter with each turn. My mother's sari is a dull red. Her eyes are also red. Is it from tears or tiredness? I do not know. She knows I am upset about something. I don't remember what it was – a lost cricket match, harsh words at school, misunderstanding, a teasing brother. I cannot bring the memory back. I only remember the stick and my mother.

"We don't know everything," she says. I look at her again. This is not something that I would expect an adult to say. These words would not fit into my father's mouth. I cannot imagine a teacher admitting ignorance or lack of knowledge. That is their job: to know it all.

"Don't expect adults to have all the answers," she says.

I am a little bit embarrassed. I scratch at the ground with my stick.

"If we knew everything, every last thing, what would there be for you to do?"

She touches my hand, stopping the movement of the stick. "Life is a mystery far from being solved."

My mother had a way. She knew when to speak. She knew when I was listening.

RAIN

The rain I saw in Nargol on that day so many years ago was unlike any rain I had ever seen before. Or since.

In India, the monsoons are monsters. But they are predictable monsters – to be avoided, but not feared. Their arrival is on a fixed date, a feast day, the arrival of a god, welcomed although not always praised. The monsoon is a solid wall of water, a purification. We know its nature.

In Vancouver, where I sit now, contemplating the years now passed, the rain is like drab wallpaper. It is there, but ignored in all its grey dullness. Like Nargol, this rain comes in off the western ocean, but in degrees and variations – intermittent showers, isolated showers, scattered showers, drizzle, mist, all words to describe the same thing: rain, water from the sky. It is all the same, whether a sprinkling or a downpour.

The people in Canada ignore the rain like they ignore so many other things. Umbrellas are communal property, shared and discarded, infrequently purchased. Rain happens, as they say. It is just a backdrop to the rest of life. In Vancouver, life is lived under an umbrella. We are protected from so much.

But that rain in Nargol was like nothing else. Not a wall, not a sprinkling shower. That rain in Nargol, in my memory, now so often revisited like a familiar bookstall – a favourite volume reopened, a single illuminated page viewed again for the nine hundredth time – was a gentle rain. It was like light falling in the form of rain. Slanting lines, soft, refreshing. It was an announcement that had nothing to do with the clouds or the air or meteorology. That rain was like an eclipse. It eclipsed the cricket match. It eclipsed my thoughts. It fell in one place like a spotlight focusing all attention. It circled me in waves and took me beyond my own life.

EGGS

"Ande wallah." I didn't have an alarm clock or a rooster. There were no nightingales in Nargol. If I slept through the morning birds, Mr. Patel would wake me. "Ande wallah." That was his call. Down the length of our street he walked alone. He pulled a small wagon or sometimes he had just a basket to his shoulder, adjusted for whatever little comfort the weight would allow. Sometimes he had both wagon and basket.

"Ande wallah." There was no beckoning in his voice, no salesmanship or life. If you were a stranger to our street, you might question what his indifference was telling us. Like a dhyal or magpie-robin repeating the same call over and over, marking its territory, calling for a mate or marking the time of day, Patel was there every morning. He didn't need to list or detail the wares he was offering. He had said it so many times, worn the words down to their barest, their exact pronunciation was no longer important. Their meaning continued.

If he had just bellowed nonsense syllables or animal noises, it would have been enough. He could have called, "I am here" or "Patel-patel" or anything. We would have translated it the same. "Ande wallah" meant "eggs seller," but now bitten and chewed by his last few teeth, he gave us the essence, sort and sharp. Patel sold eggs. He also tried to sell bread.

To me ande wallah meant "get up."

I woke. No stretching, no washing. My age didn't demand it. Trousers, shirt – one, two. I ran to the street. Left, right, no Patel. But there, in the morning light, at the temple gate: Patel!

I do not know if Patel was his name. I never called him that directly. I wouldn't have known how to address him – perhaps uncle or sir. I never spoke about him to anybody really, not even his customers. I had no need for a name. I just gestured down the street in his direction. "He says eggs are fresh," I might say. But in my mind he was Mr. Patel. It was painted, faded now, on the side of his wagon: "Patel's."

"Eggs," I called down the sloping road as I saw him in the dimness. Maybe that was his real name – Mr. Eggs. "Eggs, sir." My running slowed to a trot as I approached the temple gate.

His attention was directed inwards, through the gate, towards the small courtyard. He dusted his hands and turned.

"Eggs. Eggs. Sir." I repeated my words as my breath would allow. I didn't want to buy eggs and certainly not bread. Who wanted bread in all of Gujarat? Maybe the long gone British or a few who thought themselves to be rajahs.

I didn't want to buy. I wanted to sell. On most mornings before school and more often on non-school days, I helped Mr. Patel with his deliveries to the thirty or so houses on our street and around the corner on the lane towards the school. Perhaps he knew I was honest. Or more likely, he knew I could do the arithmetic, take the money, count the change, deliver the eggs unbroken. The easy math meant I would not make careless mistakes. My honesty was a bonus. Mr. Patel paid me with two hard-boileds, maybe a bit discoloured or undersized, but still a good breakfast.

On that day, I was there to help and to eat, as always. But in my heart I also wanted to tell him about what I had seen at the beach. Among all the people I knew, Patel seemed the wisest. The aura of wisdom grew from his few well-chosen words. The little he did say mattered. Patel was also older than most. He had known the Quit India Movement. He had fought the British – with eggs maybe. I had the idea he had even been in one of their prisons, tortured like a hero. I was too shy to ask him about the scar on the side of his nostril. A knife-wielding guard, a sword fight to defend Hindustan. It was like a victory medal worn with honour.

Patel was wise, without doubt. I had seen the way he touched the ground before the temple gate as he passed each day. It seemed that Patel knew the Gods, or at least their ways. If not in actual con-versation with Krishna and Rama, maybe he might have their ear.

I ran from house to house. I met the mothers at the doors. I tapped lightly at the windows. Each house had a different rule. "Three eggs wrapped in paper. Bread is good too, if you want." "Eggs are fresh. Uncle knows every chicken. They only give their eggs to him, so he can find them a good home."

At the end, Mr. Patel handed me my two eggs. He smiled warmly. He seemed – not tired, but different. The world was a heavy burden.

I didn't know how to open the subject of the beach and the rains and the feelings I had had seeing the woman, the calm centre of a storm. At the school, the teacher just changed the subject whenever he wished or when the wall clock told him. "Now finish with your numbers, we are on to spelling" was the command. With Patel, I did not have that kind of confidence.

I held my breath, an egg firm in each fist. "The beach yesterday...." There was no turning back. He was looking at me. "It was raining at the beach, but nowhere else. There was wind, but nothing was moving. The birds were quiet, hushed. Yesterday I saw."

It all came out in a tumble. As I said it, it became more real. Like a dream retold, the telling gave it importance. Meaning sprouted in every detail.

He looked at me slowly, deeply. He touched my arm, giving me another egg. "I saw her also," he said. "There was peace in the air and in my heart."

"Who...?" I said, thinking about the woman.

"I don't know, but I will ask until I meet her."

He turned, as he did every morning to continue his route, leaving me to follow the lane towards the school. Patel turned back, facing me fully.

"The temple knew nothing of her," he said.

BEACH VISIT

It was with both reverence and caution that I approached the spot where the woman had sat. Back a bit from the beach, sheltered by the leaning trees, but still open to the fresh sea breeze, I considered it as something like a holy spot. Sacred ground.

At first, I was unsure if it was the woman or the event that made the place holy. It had seemed from where I had been, up the hill a bit, on the footpath, that all the attention of the world had been focused there. But maybe it was the woman who was drawing my attention in such a singular way.

I walked a bit sideways, three, two, then just one step at a time, gauging the air temperature, the relative calmness of the wind, reading and counting whatever I could measure. But there was nothing to count, only a sense, a feeling and a memory.

"Here. No, it was here she sat." I felt the ground with my foot, slipping off the chappal and kicking it gently to one side. I couldn't tell for sure, but I was close. I followed the feeling, digging my toe into the warm earth.

I sat. I placed the flat of my hand on the ground without thinking. "I want this." I heard myself say the words. No one else was there to hear. "This I want."

I had only intended to look and go. Cricket would be starting soon. Some boys were probably gathering already, waiting for the arrival of the wickets. The day was beginning, a day like all the others.

In the distance some people were walking on the beach. Two men approaching a third. Some birds, large seagulls, floated in the air, occasionally dipping, repositioning. There was some shouting, distant and close at the same time. It was the boys tossing a ball, preparing for a game, teasing, name-calling, laughing. It was also the gulls, cawing and crying. I was with them all – men, boys, birds – as I still sat beneath the tree. And I was also separate. I was detached and I was motionless. My palm still touched the Mother Earth. Without thought or desire, without past or future, I felt one thing: "This I want." But "this" had no name. It was everything.

MEETING

Patel's words surprised me in a way. It was not what he said, but the length with which he spoke, the number of words he used, the time spent speaking without economy or reserve. Usually it was just a nod or a smile or a sentence of minimum length. "Take the eggs." "Hold this now." "Sell some bread. Try."

On this day he told a story.

"Near the beach road," he said. "She was staying there. Now she is gone."

I looked at his eyes. I could see that he was trying to tell me more than the words would actually allow. The language was inadequate.

"I asked until I was told," he said. "She is from Maharashtra somewhere. She stayed and now she is gone. The neighbour man told me where to knock."

His words were not just a retelling or a remembering. He was not reporting or shortening. I was there with him, as he told me.

Patel approaches the bungalow. His knock is short, sharp, polite. He carries no eggs. His white cap is removed, held in his hand. Once proudly worn, the sign of a new independent India, he now wears the cotton cap as a simple protection from the hot sun. He holds it now with both hands, nervously wringing it. He stands to his full height, his aged back straightened with respect. He waits. He is patient. The door opens. A woman in a white sari smiles deeply. She looks at him and then beyond. "Who else was approaching?" he thinks, quickly looking behind.

"I was at the beach." He looks down when he speaks to her. "I saw you. Yesterday morning. I want...."

"I am not giving yet. Soon. Maybe."

"I want," he repeats a little louder, but with dignity and respect, firmness, humility. "I want what you are giving. The moksha. The peace. Is it connection? I am an old man now. It has been a long time."

"I will find you," she promises. "Soon," she says. The last word is a seal attached to her promise.

The woman's face is comforting. She has an assurance that comes from wisdom. Her presence is a protection.

Patel bows deeply. He reaches to touch her feet.

"I told her I will wait," Patel said to me. He held the egg out to me. "These eggs we sell do not get the chance to be reborn as chickens. I want the rebirth. I want another chance."

I could hear the train. A distant chugging and a whistle, long and low. Patel could wait. He was an old man, an old spirit in an old man's body.

I didn't know if I could wait with him. Life turns and shifts in ways you don't expect. Doors don't so much open as slide, revealing and hiding at the same time.

One day I would be on that departing train. I wondered where it would be going.

STORE

Like Patel, my father had a store: Darshane's Dry Goods. Unlike Patel's travelling shop, my father's store was not on wheels. Patel went to his customers, delivered door to door. My father's business relied on the customers finding him. Maybe that was the problem.

Darshane's Dry Goods was firmly anchored, beached and stranded in the tideless lagoon of a side street with little foot traffic and even fewer cars. The customers were not many, but they were loyal – as long as they didn't find a better price. My father tried his best to please. "Come back tomorrow, we will have it for you," or "Wait just a moment, the boy will run and get." That boy was usually my older brother, but sometimes, when he was occupied, it was me.

"Run to the pharmacy, not the L & A, the other one on the corner," my father said to me, "take this note, get the Neem toothpaste, the big one, run or the customer will not wait next time." Father turned back to the customer. "The boy will be fast. Do you need a toothbrush? These just arrived, very modern. Everyone in Bombay has."

My job was to run swiftly while my father kept the customer occupied, but there was a limit how long he could hold his catch. My running was not very fast, but at least I was not distracted, not slowed by anything except my legs. There and back, dodging people and taxis, quickly, quickly, Neem toothpaste only, in the door, out the door. Still, as much as I tried to be the sprinter, the relay runner with his Neem baton, I could see my father looking for me when I returned. Fast, but not lightning fast like my brother.

The dry goods of the store name seemed to suggest anything that was not wet. In truth, my father stocked anything that he could sell, the smaller the better, so as to fit into his small shop, a sliver in the line of other stores that filled the street one end to the other. To reach up high, he would use a wooden stool with fold-out steps, knocking and poking with a long stick. Down would fall a package of combs or a bundle of pens – plonk, directly into his hand. Breakable or heavy things were stored near the floor. The more exotic or unpopular, the higher they went. Who knew what might be on that last shelf near the ceiling beyond the rotating arms of the electric fan.

SAT

Sat did not go to my school. When I think back on it, I don't think he went to any school – ever. It would be hard to imagine Sat in a classroom. The two things just didn't go together: Sat at a desk in a row with other boys. Sat in a line, tallest to shortest, alphabetical, smartest to dumbest. "Now, Satyajit, what is 12 times 7? Repeat."

Sat's mind didn't work that way. Hallways and staircases, permission slips and report cards were not of his world. Sat's poetry was not something to be memorized – or even written.

I never went looking for Sat. He always just appeared – on a hilltop, distant and calling, at my back with a surprise and a laugh. He always had something in his hand – a knotted string, a plastic stick, a bit of found something. His speech always arrived in mid-sentence as if he was always talking to himself and only sometimes did the underground stream bubble out.

"...on the tracks, you flatten the coin, punch a hole through it, string, like a bracelet, like a garland, sell it, like that...."

People probably didn't trust Sat. He didn't know what twelve times anything was. That wasn't his way. Sat knew people. He knew when they were not looking. He knew back doors and how to mend things. He knew when to use a smile, when to mention a name, when to be invisible. Sat could make a cricket ball out of rags and string and elastic and mud for glue. Sat knew the world. He knew how the gears turned and he could dance between their mechanical teeth.

The people who didn't trust Sat would look at him and figure he was up to no good. A boy that looked like Sat – shoes different one from the other, or no shoes, unpredictable, quick movements – was sneaky. "Where was his family? Without family, a boy will end up nowhere."

Where is Sat now? Cleaning ears at Connaught Circle in Delhi, wandering the streets, in some prison planning an escape? Sat was bold, but not calculating. Sat was spontaneous, but not impulsive. Maybe he is a politician. Maybe he is in the Congress Party or the Gujarat state government. Maybe he has adapted to the hallways of power, a hand-shaker and promise-maker. Maybe he emigrated like me, now a taxi driver in Bedford or a shop-keeper in Mississauga. I can't imagine Sat making change or counting money in a ledger or stocking shelves with Ivory soap. Maybe he is in Vancouver with me, living in a big box house on the next street. I doubt, wherever he is, if Sat is wondering where I am. But I am constantly looking for Sat. Do I expect that he will wave to me from across the shopping mall parking lot, car keys in hand? "Whoa, Vishesh, cricket's on! I made a ball."

Sometimes Sat and I would walk the length of the broad Nargol beach south towards the river ferries. Sat was looking for things. Fishing line or floats, a useable bottle or shoe, each a component to make treasure. Whatever turned up was meant to be.

"Put there by the tide," he said. "Could be from Arabia or Africa. Or America. Floating for years for us to find. Found a shoe once. Had a foot in it." He smiled.

I don't know if Sat was telling the truth, but I wanted to believe him. I didn't literally believe him, but I knew that beneath the surface of his words there was always a truth.

"Was an American foot," he added.

I told Sat things I had learned in school. I wasn't trying to educate him. It was more like I wanted to test the ideas in the real world, the world of Sat. A kite on a tabletop is one thing, but you've got to put it in the wind to know if it is truly a kite.

"You die and then you go to purgatory for while to burn off any small sins. And then, after a time, you win your ticket to heaven. A man with a book lets you in. It's like the train station in Sanjan. You can't get on the platform without a ticket."

"I can," said Sat. "Go around with the baggage. A special door and no one watches because they're all busy. Or drinking a third cup of chai."

"Only one door to heaven, teacher says. And Peter is the big uncle who's the station master. Says Jesus died for our sins and if you're good, God's got a seat for you in heaven."

"That's nice." Sat didn't have time for sitting – anywhere. He spotted something in the sand. "Meet you in heaven, brother. No sins for me." Sat dug with his heel and then his hands. He pulled the dried and weathered wood to the surface. The sand let go and gave us a cricket bat, bleached like a bone by the sea and the sun, but still a bat. That was a good day.

ONE PRICE

What would Sat's story look like? If he could write, if he wanted to write, how would he tell his tale? A memoir, a novel, an epic poem – I think not. Sat's life is free in form, a flow that rivers on, never stagnant, a story without a beginning or end, stretching in all directions at once, unrestrained.

Would I want to read Sat's story? Would I be interested in knowing the truth of how he saw it all? Would the blue Arabian Sea be bluer still through his eyes? Would I only be interested in how he saw me? Would I skim through the pages looking for my own name?

Would Sat even take the time to remember me, that number-loving boy with the maroon school necktie? Would he laugh at me or speak with admiration and concern?

Sat was beyond . The rulers and measuring sticks were not made for him. He just did not submit himself to their numbers.

In Sat's story, I probably would be a minor player, a member of the supporting cast, one of many. "Tonight the part of Vishesh will be played by – an understudy." No one leaves the theatre. No one regrets the switch. They are there to see Satyajit, the star.

Sat would pop up in my life at unexpected times, as if through a trapdoor or lowered by winch and rope and a bit of stage magic. I would not see him for a week, a month, a season even. I would think him dead, deported or rafting the coast in a vessel of his own invention. And then, there he was at a window, behind a door, laughing, jesting, taunting.

Sat put things in perspective. He danced in the shadows, mimicked and mimed in the corners of my life. Sat mocked authority or, more often, just ignored it.

Sat was his own master, his own teacher. And his own guru. He made his own timings and rules. Unlike me, he set the pace and step of his day. Every hour and minute was his to spend as he wished. That's how it seemed to me.

"I can't talk now, Sat. I am running for the Neem," I might call over my shoulder as I saw him at the roadside.

"Sat, Sat, do you know what homework is? If not done, they tweak on the ear. Do you want to see your friend tweaked? Do you want me to fail, repeat the grade, remain in that school another extra year? Do not condemn me to that."

"You worry," Sat would say, slowly assessing my life, "for no reason. Running is for the fool, school for the half-wit."

But there is one memory of Sat to which I keep returning. I was in my father's store. Near the back, I sat on his reaching stool. There had been no running and fetching for me that day. Customers were few. It was hot. My father gazed blankly into the street, a cup of chai in his hand.

I was happily entertaining myself with counting. The numbers gave me a comfort. I was making an inventory in a small lined school tablet:

String: seven balls

Pencils, ten times ten: one hundred

Baby bibs, blue: three

Baby bibs, green: one

Like that, I was happy. On the opposite page I recorded the unit price and the total price. On the rest of the page I was plotting to include my father's profit, loss and investment return. Charts and graphs, discount prices, fluctuating prices would follow.

"Father, how much do you pay for these bibs?" I asked him. He didn't hear. Still he was staring at the street.

"If all bibs are sold, do you buy more and in what quantity?" No answer.

A man entered the shop. He was a foreigner, a person of some wealth and income perhaps. "Do you have a kurta?" He asked.

My father's trance ended. A sale. At last.

"A kurta-pyjama," the man said. The sale grew in size. Maybe more than one set? The man, in Western clothing, looked hot. Clearly, he was looking for something cooler to wear.

"Yes, sir." My father stood up. "Many to choose from. Top export quality." He clapped his hands in my direction indicating that I should fetch. "For you?" he asked, eying the man's size.

"Yes. Three. Cotton. And a fourth in silk."

Shirts and especially old style kurtas were not sold often. Other stores had a better selection. But that did not stop my father. He believed that a good store should have everything and, if not everything, then a fast-footed boy to fetch. "Do you need an umbrella? The boy will fetch, no problem." The few kurtas that we had in stock were kept in a basket tethered to the ceiling. A string was threaded through a pulley. I loosened the string at its hooked anchor and lowered the basket.

"Very fine," my father began. Everything in the store was very fine, top or export quality, sometimes even "number one Oxford Street" depending on who was being spoken to. He held a kurta up to the customer, pinning it to his shoulders with his fingers and then measuring the sleeve against his arm. "Perfect," he concluded. "Not even in Delhi could you get such quality as this."

The man felt the kurta material between his fingers. "Cotton?" he asked.

"One hundred percent. Such is not even available in Delhi. Hand spun. Village quality. Khadhi." My father wanted this sale. "Genuine article," he added.

"And the silk?" the man asked, looking towards me and the back of the shop.

"The boy can run and get."

"There is no need." The man waved his head, Indian style, in a noncommittal way, weighing his options.

"The boy can run."

"I will take these."

"Some ice coffee while you wait?"

I stood, shoes on my feet, set to go. I waited for my father. His word would be the starter's pistol.

"How much?" The man had his wallet out and was counting.

My father motioned for me to sit down. He wrote some numbers on a piece of paper, multiplying and adding.

"The same as everyone else." The voice came from above.

Together everyone looked up. It was Sat cross-legged, perched on one of the upper shelves, like a guru on a Himalayan peak. He had been there the entire time listening.

"Give him the same price you give everyone else." Sat's words drop like bombs from heaven. "Just because he is a foreigner, does not make it right that you over-price."

My father tried not to look embarrassed. His recovery was quick. "Ignore him." He waved his hand so much as to dismiss Sat as an illusion. "He is a pest. He is a street boy. Knows nothing."

"What will he think of our country if you charge one price to the housewife and three times that to the visiting tourist? What will he say of us when he gets back to his home?"

I watched intently. My father was silent, unsure whether to argue or to ignore.

"One price for all!" Sat declared. His voice, a rally cry, was beginning to get attention from the street. "Next a surtax for out-of-towners, Mr. Darshane?" someone called from the street.

"The boy is right," my father said quietly, squashing the paper in his hand. "And I will add in a nice fan to cool the heat. At no extra cost. And maybe some ice coffee now?"

Satyajit's sense of justice was uncompromising. He was above it all.

FATHER SPEAKS

I have five children. Three boys, two girls. Each is dear to me. Five stars in the sky. My family is a constellation. Each is a part of me, but different again.

The eldest is Ravindra. Unlike me, he is a leader. But like me, he knows the rhythms of life. He knows human nature. He is a master of many things. When Ravi enters a room everyone notices. But more than that, Ravindra knows the room. He creates security and purpose for those around him. For a long time Ravi was our only child. I expect, he will one day be taking the reins of our family.

Adinath is second. His birth was a blessing to us. He is artist. I have never taken brush in hand or even mastered a photo beyond a snapshot of family arranged in rows, all smiling the same smile, but I know the pleasing arrangement of colours. I place the combs and brushes hanging in my shop so that together they will make a rainbow, gently moving through the hues of colour. The customers might not notice, but they will feel. I can feel art, but Adinath can express it. He is sensitive and knows how to use that sensitivity to make a better world.

The two youngest are the girls. They honour me by their very presence. They sweeten the smallest moments of life as they serve food to my plate or greet a new day. Gauri speaks with the tender words of a mother, even though motherhood is years away. She might be a teacher one day and she will teach the world to love.

Jagruti knows the sweep of life. "Daddy," she says, "we only learn so to get us through our life. To drive a car, to cook a meal serves us now, but the things of value are the skills, the knowledge that we will take beyond this life." Jagruti is wise. She is me and she is not me.

And then there is Vishesh. Sometimes I think he is my dearest. He is in the middle. I know him better than I know myself, but then the next moment I know him not at all. He is a puzzle. He cannot run. But he can serve a customer without confusion. Yes, he can count, add the numbers in his head with an effortless ease, but sometimes I feel he is not of this world. I don't know if he has the clarity of vision, but he is always looking – mostly in the distance, beyond the horizon, behind the stars. Vishesh talks to everyone and that is a problem too. He is too friendly with the street boys and the old men of the temple with their old ways. Vishesh talks to everyone because he wants to know their truths. He is curious and he is cautious. He knows there are still secrets to be discovered.

Where the other children will say "I think," Vishesh will say "I feel." That is what I notice. He will add and calculate, figure all the odds. Then he will feel. The feeling is the thing he believes.

Sometimes I fear for Vishesh. Sometimes I think that he will not be able to run when trouble comes. But then, I look at him and I see the future. There is a new world in Vishesh's eyes. Vishesh is not a dreamer. That is my way, as I sit staring into the street. Vishesh will make his own path. He is an explorer who will discover new lands, whole new worlds unknown to his father, a shop-keeper on a back street in an unknown city, in a country misunderstood.

They say that if a man has both a son and a daughter, then he is a millionaire. In that case, I am a millionaire twice over and then I also have my Vishesh as a bonus, a prize that cannot be counted in rupees or dollars or pounds. Vishesh is a strongbox containing untold treasures, a gem in the crown of the Gods. As are all my children.

CUP

My father had a cup. Cheap china white with a gold trim around the ring edge, I remember. There was a suggestion of a rose on the side, faded and lifeless. I think it was a rose, but perhaps a thistle or even a chakra wheel like the one on our flag. Time and memory can swap detail for detail. As the truth fades, the next best thing replaces it.

What I do remember with certainty is my father's hand. That is where the cup was kept, the rose-thistle-chakra-wheel sheltered from the sun, his hand warmed by the tea. Or more often, the tea, tepid and half drunk, was warmed by the wrap of his hand.

To say my father loved that cup might be going too far. He loved many things: his shop, his cricket, his country, his wife and I suppose even his children when they did well at school or excelled on the cricket field or ran fast for a tube of toothpaste or hair oil. The sweep of my father's love probably did not extend as far as that teacup, but more than once I did witness his upset and bother if that cup was misplaced. Everything stopped. The store was as good as closed until that cup was found, refilled and restored to his palm. He did not love that cup, but it was his closest companion. His touch was tender, protective and nurturing. The cup served.

I must explain what I mean when I say shop or store when I talk about Darshane's Dry Goods. You are probably imagining a building with aisles and shelves, show-windows with signs and prices and in-vitations to buy. My father's shop was not like that. Forget what you know. Imagine a single counter facing a road, a single tube light of-ten flickering green with age, floor space for two customers, a couple more if they are children or if they squeeze in tightly. If you came to my father's shop for a package of cotton lamp wicks or scented shampoo, you might have to stand outside and wait under the torn orange and white awning. Shade was good for the customers if the sun was bright and high. The awning also retained the customers in a queue if the rain was falling. Like the cup, the awning served, but my father also sold umbrellas if the big drips spilling over the edge of the tear were too much.

Looking inside the shop, you will see my father seated at the short counter, cup in hand, newspaper cricket pages spread. Beyond you might see your shampoo on one of the popular-item level shelves. That's me in the very back, happy not to be running, pencil in hand, now spinning the shampoo bottle, counting how many times it points north, south, east, west.

As the customers wait, a boy in the street with small clay cups and two plastic glasses walks slowly. He is selling tea. He does not need to call "chai." He rings a bell, clear and sharp. It is understood by all, an invitation to stop working. His chai varies in quality, sometimes weak, sometimes strong, sometimes sweet, sometimes spiced by the dust of the road. My father takes a refill. His hand does not loosen.

"This shampoo wants to travel west," I am thinking. When everything is a contest, even a bottle of Amla gooseberry gets to vote. Shampoo is a Hindi word, our gift to the English language, like thug and bungalow. The English with their hats and umbrellas, perhaps they did not wash their hair until they came here. They probably did not even rest on the shaded verandah of their summer bungalow in Bengal. Even when seated, they were still hunting the tiger. And in their perfect kingdom far away, they never knew what to call a gang of thieves – until they visited Hindustan. "Here, sahib," we said, "you can have our word thug for those rascals. It is a small word. You can call it quickly. See – 'thug, thug.' It is our gift to you. Take it home if you need to use it."

I laugh to myself. "Good joke, Vishesh. Tell us another."

The English – they gave us trains and bureaucratic paperwork. We gave them a new word to call a crook and taught them how to wash their hair. Three hundred and fifty years they were in our country, but who's counting? We gave them the good with the bad, theirs to sort out which was which. Khakis and karma. Typhoons and yoga. Pundits and pyjamas. Our language was rich with the names for things they had never seen. What did they sleep in before they met us? Rupees and rice, namaste and nirvana. We had it all. And it was all theirs for the taking. To me, it was a fair trade. For all that, we got the trains. And the cricket too!

"Shampoo – it means to rub hard," I am thinking. I rub the side of the bottle. Again I spin it. Again it points west.

"Where is it!?" My father is shouting. It is too hot to shout. I jump, ready to run. Is it to be a box of matches or a box of marbles, a special brand of something of no special interest to anyone but a fat auntie?

"It is gone!" my father shouts. "Again it is gone."

I know better than to offer my father another cup and a fresh serving of chai. There are more cups in a box near the floor. They are waiting to be sold, but to him there is no other cup. He wants his cup, china white and cheap, so I start looking. The finding is not so important right now as is the action, the looking under the papers, behind the cans and boxes. I match his shouts with quick hand movements, searching eyes. I feign concern, empathy, vexed puzzlement.

My father is now in the street. "It is that scoundrel, that thug, that friend of yours, that Sat." He spits the name and he squints down the road. "He was here with the chai cart. I saw him. He snatched my cup when I was turning the pages. He will take anything."

I had not seen Sat for several days. He had been there at the store that day, but I do not think he could have lifted a cup from the grasp of my father's hand. My father's certainty makes it a "maybe so" in my mind. My father's way was to blame the most convenient culprit, whoever came to mind without too much thinking.

"He is not to be trusted. That boy is a, is a...." My father did not finish his sentence. He did not know what Sat was. Neither did I. He only knew his cup was gone.

When I saw Sat a few days later, I said to him without introduction, "My father thinks you have his cup." It was not an accusation or a demand for its return. It was just information. He could do with it as he wished. "His white chai cup –vanished," I explained, making it sound more like a magic trick than a theft. "Poof." I snapped my fingers.

Sat shrugged his shoulders, as much as to say, "Why are you telling me?"

"He made me look everywhere," I offered.

"Didn't do it." Sat was indifferent.

The thing about Sat was that he knew himself. His confidence was not false. He knew. He didn't care what others thought because he knew different. It was okay for a shopkeeper to call him a thief or even a thug or a goon because he knew fact. His shrug was not a confession. It was a surrender of no contest.

Sat was steady. Unlike the teachers at the school or the brahmin at the temple, Sat did not impose his standards on others. He kept to himself and his measuring stick was of his own making. It was designed only for Sat to judge Sat. It was only to be read by Sat himself.

In a way, Patel explained all this to me when he told me why we needed very much to meet that lady we had seen on the beach.

"Vishesh," he said, "how are you ever going to understand others unless you understand yourself?"

It was not a question that required a reply. It was logic. He could as easily have said, "How are you going to climb the stairs without ascending the first step?"

PATEL RETURNS

I ran into Patel a few years later. I think I had pretty much completed my schooling, teetering on the edge, anticipating my new freedoms in a wider world. With certainly, I wanted over that fence. But also feeling the first pressures of career and commitment that would soon come, I wanted to also keep one hand on the railing, retaining a bit of the world I knew. Cricket and egg deliveries just a bit longer, please.

In that moment when a boy is asked, "What will you be when you grow up?" the bubble of childhood is popped. Don't ask that question. Games and pretend and the eternal now all naturally come to an end. Don't hurry it along. My mother never asked. "When you grow up you will be happy," was her only prediction, never a question.

At least I was not our family's oldest son. The weight of that responsibility was a shadow on my brother. The store, our father and his expectations quickly made Ravi a serious and correcting sort, no longer the brother I had long known.

When I saw Patel, he was pushing a bicycle. A box and several bags were tied to the frame and handlebars with thick, knotted rope. He was crossing the empty cricket field. I was on foot also, but without the weight of a heavy bike to slow me down. I did not recognize Patel at first, although outwardly he had probably changed very little. It should have been me who defied recognition, having moved from childhood to almost an adult, taller, lankier, no longer a boy.

"Vishesh," he said, a simple statement of fact. He leaned on the handlebars. His look was of affection and full attention. "Vishesh, it is me. The Egg Man."

I looked at his bike and bags. No eggs. No wagon.

"How have you been?" he asked. "I think of you often," he added in a confiding whisper.

I was taken. Why should anyone think of me except when I was standing squarely before them. What was there to think about and why do it often?

I still didn't recognize Patel fully. It wasn't that he had changed. I knew who he meant when he said Egg Man. He was familiar, but not the same. I just didn't catch the change in his face. There was nothing to compare him to. If his wagon had been in tow, I might have called in recognition, "Hello, Wagon, my old friend! How have you been? How are your wheels? Let me mend that squeak." If there had been eggs in Patel's hands, I might have known him by his job. I might have greeted the eggs, their shells and yolks. As it was, he was in the wrong place, in the wrong costume.

"Eggs..." I started.

Patel laughed in a friendly way, the laugh of a good uncle, not of a school teacher. He was ahead of me, down the path of my thoughts and questions.

"The woman was true to her word," he replied. "She kept her promise. I went to Bombay." He did not need to explain. There was only one woman.

They say that when you revisit a memory too often you change it. You analyze and test it, read details into it that just were not there in the original. An event that is forgotten for a decade and then suddenly recalled, triggered by a scented breeze or a hook of detail, is closer to the truth than something that has been fussed over, honoured with attention, mused from all angles.

This was not the case with my memory of that woman. The fact that I had been one hundred percent in the present as I watched her from the grove of beachside trees welded the memory intact, unchangeable. Whenever I thought of it, I was there.

"The woman was real," I heard him say again. "In Bombay I met her again. She is like no other."

"Everyone is unique," I thought. "Sat is like no other." I was silent.

"She makes you feel like a bird. Innocent and new. A lot of old worries fly away. She gives...."

"Patel, Patel." I used his name. "What do I do with my life now?" It was a question I should have asked my father or even my brother. It was a question that had been pressing so hard on the cage of my chest that I had to let it go. The cage door was opened. It was like a flutter of beating wings.

"Come to Bombay and I will take you to her." It was more than an invitation and also more than a promise. But it also did not seem like a job, a career or a place in the world. I was a bit confused. I was drawn to knowing more about this woman, to reuniting with Patel, but I also wanted a say in my own destiny. Sometimes things happen even before they happen because they are right. Acknowledge that and they are as good as done. But I was unsure I wanted to let go.

"I am staying at a place called Seven Sisters on Marut Road. It is near a cinema palace called the Aurora. Have you got that?"

"Yes," I said. I did.

"You have to ask for Ambika, not Patel. My name is Ambika. They will know me that way."

"Yes, Uncle."

"Ambika."

"Thank you, Uncle Ambika."

"I think she wants to see you. If you want it," he added.

AMBIKA SPEAKS

My name is Ambika. I know the boy Vishesh calls me Patel. I have been called many things in my life. Ambika is not usually a man's name, so it is good for me to have other names to hand out. Ambika means mother, so imagine the surprise when people see me with my weathered skin and scratches and scars. Sometimes I say my name is Amika. That means friend. That is a good name also.

I am reaching the end. It is time to trade in all those names in for something new, to be one with God or to be reborn and do it all yet again. Whatever I merit.

I am old suddenly. I know that people look at me and see an old man. They think I have always been old, pulling a child's wagon through the narrow streets selling eggs, but there was a yesterday when I was a child, a boy, a young man, straight and tall. I have done those things.

I have been many people in this life. It is hard to remember them all. I fought in the army of India. I was in Burma during the war. We were helping the British to keep the Japanese out. What do I have against the people of Japan? What do I have against the British? We thought that if we helped the Englishman to fight that evil, we would be rewarded – defeat the Japanese, defeat the Hitler army and we would be given our nation back. But the war ended and we had to fight again. Quit India. Go home. I am tired of the fighting.

In the army I met my country. Men from all over, Bengali and Tamil and Punjabi eating together and we all wanted different food, each with a different language, each with a different taste. Some wanted rice, some the chapati. Some wanted chai, some coffee. When it was hot, we all wanted water. Water and the English language and the cricket brought us together. And the hope of nationhood always. With the English language we could talk to each other and learn.

So much enthusiasm for the idea of a state, so much loyalty to a piece of land, a colour of cloth on a flagpole. Like so many cricket teams, these countries, heckling each other on field and off. One day we will just say we are humans, one planet, one big team. Can you imagine what that will feel like?

I worked for the railway. I was foreman. They thought because I could tell soldiers what to do, I would also be able to tell labourers what to do. They are only loyal to their pay cheques. There is no flag to salute. We built bridges and sidings and small stations. I was given a medal by the rail company – job completed on time, on budget. A few accidents, a few injuries.

Like the army, I met my countrymen on those trains. India is a world disguised as a country. We are all different, but we call ourselves Indian. Maybe it is like that in other places as well. From far away, it looks like one country coloured the same pink on a map, but get closer and you see a family fighting. Are all Englishmen the same? Are all the Japanese like the ones we fought in Burma? I am old now. I take the world one person at a time.

When I rise from my bed in the morning, I touch the Mother Earth with the flat of my hand. "Forgive me for treading on you," I whisper. "Forgive my mistakes. May I do only your will."

I try. That is all I can do. There is no "not trying." That is death.

Surrender does not mean giving up. It is not an end to action. It is the start of worship.

The boy reminds me of myself – quick and sharp, open to new things – as I was when I was his age. I was his age once. I am still inside.

When I saw that woman at the edge of the beach, I recognized her. Did he tell you about that? It was not like the way I might recognize a customer on the street or an old army chum. It was like that small boy inside me was calling out. "Attention old man. Pay attention."

She was there at the beach, next to a tree, but it was as though the beach was there and the tree was there only because she was there. The tree was not special. The beach was not special. That woman was special.

With age something is gained. The boy thinks it is wisdom. It is not wisdom. Shri Ganesha is wise. He grants or withholds wisdom as he desires. With age the eyes begin to fail. The ears deaden to distant sounds. The legs stiffen and ache. But what you are given is clarity.

I pray every day. I pray to Lord Ram. I pray to Shri Krishna. I do not go to the temple any more. There are no answers there. Sometimes I pray at the beach. At the place where I saw her. There the sky is large and the sea reaches out to the sky in agreement. I pray for clarity: "Please, no fog, no confusion, only clarity."

I have seen a lot. I have seen a man leave this world when a bullet entered his body. I have seen my own wife die in childbirth – one arrives, one leaves. I have seen men cry with self-doubt. I have seen the Union Jack lowered and our Tricolour raised to replace it. And I have seen the partition and the cruelty that followed. I have seen a lot, so when I say that woman was like no other, you must listen. My words are few, but they come from my heart.

TRAIN

I should have been on that train, the one I could see through the window, folded, sided, smoking.

Our train slowed either with respect or with caution. We all looked. In India that is what we do: look, witness, observe the tragedy of others. Sometimes we learn, but mostly we are just hoping to see the will of God. Death is not uncommon. It is every day. No one panics, cries or turns away, unless it is their own child or spouse. It is then that the drama starts. Grief quickly blossoms into hysteria.

Tears give way to screams. The placid calm of a detached witness or unrestrained public anguish – there is nothing in between.

A billowing twist of a train, dead carriages, dying people – I should have been in there too. I was spared or graced. Or warned off. I had thrown my ticket into the toilet. Burning would have been too good, more like an offering or a ritual. I wanted that ticket to be with the filth, final and irretrievable.

I had instead chosen a later train to Bombay. It was the next train leaving, but I also, in the same moment, remembered Uncle Ambika's invitation.

That first train had been assigned passage to Pune. Both trains shared common tracks southward, not yet parted on their separate routes. Now instead, the Pune train lay on a siding of its own making, bombed. An explosion from within or perhaps from without, waiting on the tracks, halted it forever.

There was a swami or guru or rishi or, at the least, some kind of a wise man in Pune. I had heard his name. I had felt to go and see him. There had been a promise of enlightenment, a short cut to nirvana. Simplicity and wisdom were a journey away in his ashram. His pamphlets and posters had even reached Nargol. Many foreigners were going to see him, a good sign perhaps. He was a sensation not to be missed, some said. He was a saint for our times, a saint for an age when there are no more saints. Perfection was attainable in his presence – a new way and an old way at the same time.

I was twenty and unsure what I wanted. That is my excuse. Twenty seems old when you are twenty. You pretend to be mature, assured, knowing. You want to make your own decisions. Now it seems so very young.

I didn't know what I wanted, but there was one thing: change. I wanted it badly – out of Nargol, away from family, no more dry goods. I knew I would have to seek the opportunity, not wait for it to come to me.

I had bought the ticket for Pune. I had it safely, folded once, in a notebook in my pocket. I was speaking to an Australian boy, a young man of my own age. The cup of chai was too hot to drink. I wanted the taste, the first sip. I wanted it badly. I blew across the surface as I listened.

"Oh, a lot happens there all right," he said, "a lot of talking, big words, a lot of nothing. And a lot of money-taking. It's a scam if you ask me, a money-grab."

I looked, but I did not say anything. I held my notebook tight at my side pocket. Money-grab, that was a fresh way to say it. I understood.

"Go if you want," he went on, "but leave your wallet behind. If you're looking for truth, he's not the one. He doesn't look at you straight. I've seen a lot of them and I'm still hunting."

That night I had a dream. You probably expect me to say that I had a nightmare – knotted-haired gurus buried in the sand, disembodied hands sticking out, laughing, lecherous rishis counting money. Train crashes and disappointment.

My dream was simpler, not a nightmare, but it had the same effect. I dreamt of the woman at the beach. The white sari was whiter. The rain more the rain of the heavens, not the rain of clouds. The woman was even more motherly, her beauty more unique, if that is possible. My vantage point was not the same. I was somehow closer, circling, a part of it. I heard her speak, gently, directly, wisely.

I awoke, not in a sweat or with a fear. I awoke not with a jolt, but with a natural ease. I had a calm and a clarity. What she had said I could not hang on to. Like water slipping between my fingers, like incense smoke moving into sunlight, I lost the words. In the dream she had looked at me directly. The words were gone, but the feeling was clear.

I took the ticket and threw it into the toilet hole before any other ideas of the day could come to my head. Go, not there, not Pune. Truth, not imitation.

At the Sanjan station I bought passage one way to Bombay. It was my only choice. And it was the next train through. Bombay wasn't just the big city. It was Mahanagar. It was the World.

SAT SPEAKS

You don't know me. Even if you saw me, you wouldn't think much – another kid living on the street. Too bad, you almost say. And then on to the next thing. Don't waste your words.

But we are connected, you and me. You know that. Everything is connected. The sun sinks into the ocean every night, the birds skim the water so low, boys chase cricket balls on the beach. It's all the same, here or there.

My name is Sat. You know something of me if you've talked to Vishesh. He's all right, full of questions and numbers. Sat is for Satyajit. That means truth. So you better listen carefully.

Change is coming. And it's going to sweep through everything like a monsoon. Everything is going to get wet. It's going to wash away everything that is bad. There will be no more slaves and pirates and rich people counting their money. The big johnnies are going to come down fast and hard. Only the kind ones might be spared.

We are all one thing, going one way – those that want to be on the train. We're connected you and me. And if you want to stay connected, you got to be with the new way. It's an express train. No local stops allowed.

The tide comes up on the beach. Each wave is a little higher. At the top it leaves a line of garbage – sticks and seaweed, fishing stuff, plastic bottles and corks. The ocean doesn't want it. It only wants things that can become a part of the ocean. The gulls and people like me come along and pick out the bits that are useful or tasty. We're the scavengers. We sort the good from the bad.

You've got to want to be a part of the ocean. The ocean is the biggest thing in the world. And it goes way beyond the world. The sun goes into the ocean every night. The stars come out of the ocean. I am a part of that ocean too. I can feel it inside.

Change is coming. My name is Sat. You better listen. The trees, the stars, the sky, the ocean. It isn't just me talking.

AMBIKA SPEAKS

When I told Vishesh about meeting the woman, I did not tell him everything. Words cannot say everything. And even if there are words, the meaning can slip between. You can end up talking and talking but saying nothing. Some people want to fill in every bit of air with their words. What is the use?

This woman was different – different from all the rest, different than anyone. I told Vishesh this, but he did not listen. Not fully.

She was different than me, but at the same time she was me. I saw in her my mother, my child, my self. She took me out of time and put me right back into it again, as if no other place, no other moment existed. How do you say those things to a child?

In Nargol, she told me to wait. She said that she was not ready yet to teach. She said soon. Soon can mean a lot of things. The English said soon and that turned into many years. They lost our trust with their delays and tricks. But her I trusted when she said soon.

She asked where I lived. I said, "Just near, I live now right here in Nargol." I said that I had once lived in Calcutta. With large eyes and full attention, she said I had come a long way, fully across the country.

I don't think she was meaning just the journey across India. That had been easy. I think she meant the journey of my life that brought me standing now on her doorstep.

BOMBAY

I was not prepared for the city. In those days, we still called it Bombay in the British fashion. It was a magnet that drew people from across India – a magnet that didn't let go. Oh, Bombay, city of dreams, or at least a city in which to chase dreams: money, fame, vibrant shops with plentiful customers, your face painted two stories high, a billboard hoarding advertisement for the latest from the Bollywood dreamwala – the greatest story ever told, until the next one, everything in one movie, something for the entire family.

Taken in detail, Bombay was a brightly ticking clock. Taken in parts, neighbourhood by neighbourhood, sections and precincts, it supported life with services and faces as familiar as those in our little corner of Nargol. Now that I have seen more of the world, I know to say that most large cities are like that: a collection of neighbourhoods united under the banner of a global name, a brand. Only from a distance does it appear to be one, a pretty mosaic. Up close it is a mess.

Travelling across Bombay, trying to find the Aurora Cinema, Marut Road and then hopefully the Seven Sisters, it seemed to me that the city was the same thing again and again. I was running within a wheel: another Bata Shoes, another Laxmi Tailor, another Shivaji International Travel, or another variation of the same – different name, same signage. The toot-tooting three-wheel auto-rickshaw taxis were like drone bees, yellow-black insects, delivering, pollinating, maintaining a city.

A train, a bus and a couple of these taxis brought me to the Aurora in the late afternoon. I was tired. It was the heat, the sitting and, for me, the lack of ocean air.

"Marut Street," I said through the slitted glass of the ticket office. The woman, not looking at me, pushed a ticket half way towards me, pausing for money before advancing it the rest of the way. I was just so tired. I looked at the sign beyond her in the lobby: in English "AIR CONDITIONED," each letter capped in cartoon snow. The lobby oasis invited me. Across the steel counter, my money met her hand. I took my ticket and stepped inside. I bought a sweet mango drink in a tall glass bottle. "Anything that is cold," I said.

I took my place, downed the drink. I was asleep.

It was the combination of a padded seat, the mechanically overcooled air and the darkness. While others outside were chasing their dream, I was fully within mine, at home, my world only occasionally nudged by a sound from the screen or the jostling of the people around me.

DREAM

The sleep I had in the Aurora Cinema was deep. It was more than a sleep. It was an escape, a departure from the world. Perhaps it was infused and directed by the happenings on the screen or maybe I was just permitted to fantasy by the world of cinema. It all happened in a flash, but also seemed to last and sustain, a complete empire.

I walked on a wide field that slowly waved with each step I took, like a blanket being shaken so slowly, ripples and waves, unseen hands. Cricket balls shot past me, each closer to my shins or ankles, threatening to bruise or break. I walked faster.

Voices filled my ears and mind. "Take the train." "Eggs and bread." "Fetch the Neem." "Seven to the power."

A white-white bird with black bead eyes circled and circled again higher. Something from its claws dropped, falling towards me, faster. A cricket ball, hard and dirty. I held my hands in front of my face to protect, to shield my eyes from the sun. My hand was open. A hit, but not a ball. An egg unbroken.

"Run, you will score." "Run, run, the customer is waiting." "Run, you are late for school." "Bow at the temple gate." "The wicket is down." "The train is leaving." "Faster, run."

And then: quiet, quiet calm. Nothing on the wide field. Light from all directions. The blanket pulled tight. A woman in a white sari. The sky is a red-pink shawl.

A rain is falling, but it is gentle, warm, not wet. The sun shines from all directions, warm, without burn. The wind blows, but like a voice, not a storm. A whisper to my ear.

I stand and reach forward. There is something just outside my reach. It is there, but I cannot see it. The sun is in my eyes, so I close them. Tight, but there is still light.

I hear a voice. Not Hindi. Not English. Clear and sweet. "A long way, but not far."

I open my eyes. Slowly. The sun is bright. But it is not hot. The sea breeze is cooling us now. The tide rises to touch our feet, a friend reaching out, regular, predictable, something to rely upon

The children are playing and I am one of them. I am aware of my life from beginning to end, all of it. I have lived it out and I am living it still. This life and the many lives, as much as they are all mine, I am not that.

These children around me are also me. Many are one. I hold a red knotted thread in my hand. It rises to the still sky like a kite string. It disappears in the vastness, in the blueness. Still I hold it. It connects.

I look again. I hold many threads. Each is connected to another child, who holds the thread as the play continues. I am he. I am she. I am each of them. The threads are the warp and weft that make the fabric, single threads together, a textile of bright design, bold with colour and pattern, a beautiful shawl.

Who am I? The question is drowned out by the sound of the waves rifting, white with surf, falling on the shoreface, drawing back, sucking at the rocks of the beach. And, in turn, the waves are covered by the cries and cheer of children. We are that.

We play with pebbles, collecting and scattering. We play with shells, small. We weave our play ships from leaves. The sun warms us. We share the warmth on that endless beach. Together.

We know nothing of war, nothing of argument. Harsh words, doubt and fear have no place on that beach. At no moment did our play begin. It does not know of end. And still we are there, the sun warming and protecting.

I try to hang on to the feeling. The moment evaporates as I awake.

•

Awake: one sense at time. The eyes are last. My hand is reaching out towards the movie screen. I pull it back. What will the people think? But the cinema is empty. I am alone. How much time has passed? The screen is dark, empty.

I grasp at the threads drifting away. I try to recover as much as I can, but it is gone. The voice, the egg, the wind and rain are not of this place. The beach is somewhere so close, so real, but not of here. I look and half expect sand and water at my feet. I look for children, but there are none. Their laughter is gone. There is an electric hum.

I rise and stumble, my leg cramped and unsure. I am in two worlds. I want to be in just one. There is no going back, so I go forward.

It was as if I had been away a hundred years. It was as if I had been travelling, returning from a long adventure only a moment after I had left. The cinema is dark and vacant. The movie long over, the audience and projectionist gone.

In the empty lobby, I found a door through which I could exit. I heard its clicking lock behind me. The street was quiet. A rat scampered in the distance, crossing before me, from darkness to darkness.

Still half in another world, I walk the streets. I did not even bother to look back to the dimmed marquee to see what movie I had missed. Even if there had been light to see, I don't think I would have been interested in the black and red plastic letters mis-spelling the title and its stars. But now, I wonder.

The sounds and even the images from that film must surely have reached into my sleep, into my dreams, colouring their tone, infusing the drama with sound effects and underscoring the action with their music. It might have been *Kalyug* or *Umrao Jaan*. The year was right. Or perhaps it was another revival showing of *Sholay* or even *Mother India*. I muse at the mystery: perhaps *Ghare-Baire* – known to me now as *Home and the World*. Who knows? It could even have been *Gandhi* for all the crowds and shooting and shouting, the drama that entered my ears. Or *Star Wars* for that matter. Triumphantly, I would have liberated the nation – or the princess – whatever the screenplay demanded.

As I walked, it was the second dream to which I clung. It was not a dream, not in the same way. It was not a mixing, a confusion, a river of events tearing past me all in the same moment. It was a calm oasis from within, the place I wanted to be.

I did not return to a bed that night. I walked the streets alone until the first light of morning. My mind was filled with possible worlds. Bombay was a magnet sucking at me. I wanted to be free.

the stars are the only constant

You can't cross the sea
merely by standing and staring at the water.

Rabindranath Tagore

REFLECTION

I do not know why I am telling you all this. Maybe I should stop here and let you imagine the rest, but somehow my life does not take the trajectory that you might expect: idealistic boy, optimistic youth, hard-working immigrant, disillusioned mid-lifer, reflective and resigned elder.

What are we here for, this same cycle of struggle and disappointment over and over?

Somehow I was determined that it would all be different for me. Doesn't everybody? I wanted more. At my darkest moment, hope reached up from the deepest well.

At twenty, had I already felt it all? Was the rest just going to be a pale reflection of the past? Ascent is the only real achievement, the only real goal.

I wanted more. I knew that hoping was not enough. I knew that wisdom had to be real, but I also wanted to be a lot more than a wise old owl, respected by the chickadees and ducklings, spouting wisdom and advice for all, but knowing nothing for himself, respected simply for his age, because he has survived.

I still wanted to be the nightingale announcing the new day.

SHARMA

When opportunity knocked, I answered the door. When freedom called, I shouted back. I wish that was true. The fact is that Bombay sucked me in and spat me out the other end before I knew it. Looking back, I don't think the decision was mine, no matter how much I was in charge and making the decisions.

I left India. It was a simple act. Like stepping through a doorway or crossing a small bridge, it was done. It was a threshold like any other. Was it an impulse or a plan? It's hard to remember whether I jumped blindly or was waiting for the opportunity.

But this I know: just because you are holding an oar doesn't mean you are navigating the boat. The current usually makes most of the decisions. So it was with me. I wanted to look like I was in control. I wanted to pretend like my life was all mapped out. It wasn't. Nothing anywhere like it.

I wish I could say that my decision to emigrate was the culmination of all my dreams. It was not. At best, I can only say that I boarded that ship because, if I had not, I would have spent the rest of my life wondering "what if...."

It was like this: somehow I befriended a man named Sharma. I forget exactly how it all came about and, looking back, it was certainly an unlikely pairing. I met many people, as many as I could while I was in Bombay. Maybe I was looking for an escape and Sharma was simply the most promising. I am sure he didn't intend to be, but he was charming. And I was charmed.

He was a distinguished gentleman. In another context, you might even have thought of him as scholarly. He carried himself with a dignity that I had never seen in Nargol. Even the temple brahmin or the highest businessman or campaigning politician did not have the presence and bearing as that which was so much a part of this man. He was something I might have imagined a judge to be, had I ever had the chance to see one up close. Greying hair, but not too grey. A beard, maintained and groomed, not grown from laziness, but with care. A posture straight, but not stiff. And a formal manner in both his speech and attention that did create distance, but cultivated respect. You respected Sharma not because he was a captain, but because he respected those around him.

I called him Sharma. Everyone else referred to him as The Captain.

To get to the point of all this, Sharma was a captain in the merchant navy. It was an exotic posting for an Indian at that time, a man who left home and country for months at a go, commanding a crew of men, both misfits and professionals, all navigating and maintaining a huge freighter ship to distant and foreign ports – Doha, Dar es Salaam, Durban and beyond.

The only thing you might be wanting to say about Sharma, but then might be hesitant to bring up if you were actually standing on his ship, is that perhaps his best years were behind him. Maybe retirement was on his mind. Perhaps it was just the sheer senselessness of delivering again and again more unneeded consumables and who-knows-what-else into our country weighed him down. He said as much to me once. Overseeing the off-loading of a shipment of cheap cosmetics, bath products and the like, he slowly shook his head. "How much more of this do we need?" he muttered. "What would Gandhiji say?"

Sometimes to Sharma the names of the most familiar of his crew came slowly. Sometimes on the bridge of his ship, he gazed a bit too long at the distant horizon. Then, lowering his small telescope, he would rub his eyes and stare again.

"Show me," he might say to his first officer or navigator, waving a hand towards a map or a compass. "Is our course set? Will the weather cooperate?"

As morning moved into afternoon, he spent less time on the bridge and more in his cabin reading a chapter in a long-titled grey book. A volume of forgotten verses or maybe theories, it really didn't matter. The intention was sleep. He was soon snoring with the book on his chest and his glasses still on his nose.

In Bombay, I had taken first a job at a hotel. It seemed to be mostly a repetition of my posting at Darshane Dry Goods. It paid little beyond tips, but allowed me to watch and learn. Basically, I ran and got things for people. Sometimes I ran before they asked. "Boy, has today's Times of India arrived." I produced it from behind my back. Or holding out the evening's menu card, I might be asked, "What is on for tonight's dinner." I don't know how I did it. The simplest explanation is that, with time, most jobs become routine, even predictable. The magic is borne from the audience's perception. Among them all, it seemed to impress Sharma most.

He asked me, not so much with a question or an offer, but in a short offhand way, the way you might ask a boy to fetch a cup of tea or to open a window, to accompany him on his next voyage out. "You will be my assistant," he informed me. "My personal assistant," he added, as if he was adding a bit of jam to a piece of melba toast.

I never said yes, I never said no, but it was settled. Captain Sharma needed a personal assistant and it was to be me. I doubt if he had ever had or needed one before, the way he was always short of tasks for me to do. I polished his shoes, tidied his cabin and bedding and he even taught me how to trim his beard, which mostly involved clicking scissors in the air in a way that warned the hairs not to grow any farther. Other than that, I was generally at his side in case he needed anything and that usually meant his misplaced glasses, his pocket watch or a small snack to keep him going – raw peanuts, dried apricots or whatever I could get from the kitchen. If I simply watched and picked up everything he had put down while in a room, I could usually keep up to his requests.

"Now, that letter I was reading, from the Maritime Organization, do you think you might be able – oh, I see you have it. Good man."

Again I wasn't paid. And on the ship there were no tips and so no one to impress, but I did get food, two or three red merchant navy T-shirts, too large, and a hammock which I was allowed to string up in the passageway outside Sharma's cabin or on deck depending on the heat and weather. In a way, Sharma also paid me with his knowledge: half stories about storms or pirate threats – not the real thing, never pirates in person, no matter how much I asked, just the threats and rumours of cutthroats. The adventures of his life seemed to be most perceived – the threat of insurrection or piracy, again not the real thing. It all proved my point, reinforced something I was slowly learning: even life on the high seas can become predictably routine.

Sharma schooled me with tidbits about navigation. I loved the maps and charts, the compasses and tools. Anything he needed written down, I took a note and called him Sir. The more respect I gave, the more valued I felt.

All-in-all, Captain Sharma was a good uncle.

CREW

My age was the thing that separated me from most of the men on the ship. It was as simple as that. And easy to understand. The other gulf that divided us wasn't quite so simple or subject to measurement. It wasn't a matter of countable numbers. It was a caste division that cut two ways.

I was unskilled and so not of the same ranking as the first and second mates, navigator or engineers. The cook, who was also something of a ship's medic and so in two ways vital to everyone's survival, also outranked me.

On the other hand, my proximity to the captain, something like a favoured son or a teacher's pet, put me squarely in the upper echelons of class and privilege. There I was: an uneducated boy who knew nothing about life at sea, squarely in the pocket of the ruling elite. No doubt I was a subject for scorn and mockery. Added to this was the unorthodox way by which I had gained access to the ship – through a sort of a draft or invitational back door conveniently left ajar by Sharma – making me suspect to most and invisible to the rest.

Through careful sidestepping, repeated apology and some diplomatic maneuvering, I rose through the social ranks. From enemy alien at first, I soon became a distant but useful untouchable. Eventually, I arrived at a status we all could accept: unofficial mascot, an amusing sidekick who could get things done and, better than that, had the ear of the captain.

Through small favours, kind acts, empathy and the discrete trading of information, I became part of the family, such as it was. I was like the stray cat that everyone wanted to pet or the family dog secretly fed under the table. Looking back on it all now, I am surprised to see that within a month or so, I had successfully overcome both caste and prejudice. I was nobody's best friend, but neither was I anybody's slave.

Perhaps each crew member in their turn was taking pity on me, but it is just as likely that they were each seeing in me younger versions of themselves or a reminder of a son, nephew or younger brother left behind back home, faring without guidance. That duty – in some cases you might even call it protective love – was transferred to me. They watched out for me. All in all, I came to a place where I wanted to be: a functioning gear in the mechanism of the ship. Simply put, by taking care of Captain Sharma's smaller needs, I made everyone's life a little easier.

FOOTBALL

Every member of the crew was unique: not exactly drifters or loners, but certainly outsiders. In another age, they might have been explorers, wild men living life on the edge, in the wilderness or in a dreamtime, altering mundane realities however they chose. When I met them, they were just characters, mostly unable to function in the mainstream. I had never met their type before, but I certainly would, again and again, as the years passed.

They all had stories to tell, the whys and wherefores that had brought them to sea, insights and theories as to how the world worked or, specifically for them, didn't work. They told their tales with a zest that was served with precision. They had it figured out and they didn't mind telling just how. The only drawback was that they had all heard and told these same tales a hundred times before. Maybe this is one reason why I was able to worm my way into their company. I was a new ear, a willing audience and, above all, a good listener.

"I will tell you one thing, boy: you don't want to be looking down the business end of a knife with someone like that holding onto it."

"No, uncle, I do not. Tell me again how his breath smelled."

"Like week-old vomit. And the truth is that it probably was."

"You must have been brave to escape unharmed."

"Escaped with my life and nothing else. You can replace the clothes and the money and the other things. But your life, you gotta look after. Poof – head first out the window. There's no shame in running if you do it with honour, dignity – and speed," he laughed.

When any story-teller laughed, that was my clue to laugh too. You don't want to laugh at the wrong part, but if you listen carefully, they tell you when to laugh and when not to. I was a good listener. And a good mirror.

There was one man onboard who didn't have any stories it seemed. Not one. They called him Moseby or more often Moses for some reason. His name suggested an Englishman or maybe, I thought, an Israelite of some kind. I remembered one from school, the uncle called Moses with the stone tablets, the one who parted the sea that was red, the one with all the rules. But this Moses wasn't that sort. He spoke in what I thought was an English way, but not with the educated Indian-English of a Sharma. It was a sort of world-weary I've-seen-it-all tone. He looked Indian in his face, but he was not like any Indian I had ever met. "But," I thought, "India is a big country and I have seen very little of it." Simply put, all of these men were more like exiles or pirate-astronauts, than true patriots or land-bound citizens. They looked out for themselves and their own. They could not be contained by borders and flags. My goal, while on that ship, was to be one of them, to let them know we were all on the same side.

Sometimes, when the weather allowed, some of the men played football on the deck. "A game of friendly" they called it. Because of the ocean and low or no deck railings, this maritime venue was unsuitable for cricket. Hit it into the ocean, victory is yours every time, but no ball for the next batsman. But for football, a bit of netting and some rule changes was all that was needed. These friendlies didn't involve much strategy or teamwork. The only skill was to hit the ball into a painted goalmouth.

The area of play was not regular size, far from it. This was a freighter, a vessel of commerce, and business came first. Spare deck space was a function of our cargo capacity. Sometimes the field was irregular in shape, twisting around containers and other obstacles. Sometimes it was wide and broad as the ship rode high in the water mostly empty. But always an area was found and a football friendly was staged.

This sport filled a need for exercise beyond climbing ladders, but it was also foremost a gambling opportunity. Betting, wagering and games of chance were the favoured off-duty activities. Cards and dice were easy to find, but really anything could draw a dare, a challenge and a stake of money – a port arrival time, the size of a fish or how long a lit match could be held. The possibilities were endless.

For football, lines and goals were painted on the deck floor – rust red primer was usually the colour of choice. Teams were created, tournaments drawn, odds created, bets wagered. We played in our bare feet, cooling down the deck with a hosing.

For me, my lack of athletic skill, but impeccably impartial fairness, made me the perfect referee, rule-maker and cashier – police, judge and banker all in one. When I called a foul, a penalty kick or paid out a winning, no one argued. Fights and threats of fights were frequent, but my rulings were respected. "The boy knows, listen," was said more than once. I was the court of final appeal.

MOSES

One day, I came back from the football early. The match was not over, but I was feeling the effects of both the heat and the sea. I thought if I lay down for a bit, doused my face with water or just found a hat to cover my head, I might feel better. I was used to heat at home, but this was an unrelenting baking reflected by the metallic grey and white of the ship. I felt as if I was sitting on a skillet held over an open flame. Oh, for a cloud or an umbrella or a fresh, cool coconut.

As I made my way back towards the cabins, I hadn't decided yet which would be the best remedy – bed, hat or water. As I passed the captain's cabin, on my way towards my own hammock on a shaded part of the deck, I stopped. I was hearing a humming melody like a fly or bee, but with busy sing-song tune to it. Also, was I seeing motion inside, through the thick glass of the porthole. I knew it wasn't Sharma. I had just left him overseeing the football. He could not be back so quick. At a careful angle, I peered inside.

I couldn't be certain. The cabin was dark relative to the brightness of the deck. The glass was thick, milky with a sea brine whiteness. And the sun was still full on my head. I was not fully myself and I knew it. But in all that, there was a man alone in the captain's cabin. It was not Sharma. It was Moses.

Motionless, and also fearing that I might be seen myself and called to account, I watched with disbelief, mixed with confusion and light-headedness. Moses was looking through the captain's belongings. Carefully, slowly replacing each item as he had found it, he appeared not so much to be searching as making a studied inventory.

What was he exactly up to? I felt torn. I didn't feel in a position to challenge him – I knew him to be a fighter with a quick temper, someone who could and would seek revenge, if not all at once, certainly slowly with time. It was a long voyage and he was someone who could make it longer. But, in the end, my loyalty was to Sharma. He was my first duty on the ship. He was my captain.

Without a plan, I made my way inside, through the stepped door, along the narrow corridor and towards Sharma's closed hallway door. I knocked. No answer. I unlatched and pushed the door. Unlocked, it swung slowly. I did not enter.

"Hello?" I said. My voice was questioning, equal parts "What are you doing in here?" and "Do I have the right room, sir?"

There was nobody there. The room was empty, undisturbed. Moses, if he ever had been there, was gone. Had he taken something? I looked. It was hard to tell, but my eyes counted everything. On the surface, there was no disturbance.

Dizzy again, confused, I grasped the doorframe for support.

DILEMMA

The next time I saw Moses, I didn't know what to say. Or where to look. Not that talking, or even looking, was the usual course of events with this man – remember, he had no stories to tell and showed little interest in anybody else's adventures, especially those of a shop-keeper's son from India. A hello would get little more than a grunt, a grunt might get a shrug or a stony stare. Or nothing at all. Moses was a brick wall without a ladder.

Still, when he sat opposite me at dinner that same night, I didn't know where to look. My thoughts were filled with dark intrigues: the thievery of thugs, extortion, blackmail, mutiny. My imagination was unbounded. And Moses was the centre of all the action.

What should I do? How should I say it? "What did you find? What did you take? How did you get in? Who do you think you are?" Instead I stared at my food. I pushed it in circles around the plate. I glanced up at him only to see if he was still there, then returned to the solitude of dark thoughts. A piece of egg chased a lump of sausage around the plate, the two never meeting.

Eventually, he finished eating and left without a word. I moved to my hammock and a sleepless night.

A gentleman is a man of grace. He does not confront or insult. If he gives advice, it is in an indirect way, by example or through story. A gentleman knows when to speak and when to remain silent. He knows the limits of words, but also knows right from wrong and does not compromise one for the other. He does not move into the grey area of the in-between.

I wanted to be a gentleman, impeccable in both action and thought, a man like Captain Sharma. But I knew also that a gentleman was a man who did not worry, did not have confusion and did not lay awake at night staring at the stars while criminals slept soundly.

What would Patel do? What would Sat say? A resigned shrug and a dismissive wave of the hand. Patel might say, "Give it to God, the creator of all solutions." Sat would say, "People are like that, forget them."

"Tell me what to do," I prayed to God. "I know something is not right, but I am not sure what I saw. Is entering a crime if nothing is taken? If nothing is taken, was he even there?"

I was only a shop-keeper's son, but I wanted to be true to Captain Sharma. I wanted to do the right thing. I wanted to serve truth not convenience.

SPYGLASS

The captain lay his small telescope, a spyglass really, more show than function, back in its hinged case. The telescope often gave Sharma time to think or delay decision, while looking at the horizon, a distant ship or port. "Let me study this," he might say. Study was not really necessary with all the modern instruments we had on board. Everything was reduced to numbers and science, not the visuals and optics of a spyglass. Nonetheless, Sharma looked and studied before arriving at any decision.

"Everything as it should be" was a typical Sharma order. "As you were, men." The men didn't really have a state to go back to. "As they were" was their constant state. They did not change for crisis or high alert. In this respect they were solid.

We were off the coast of east Africa, Tanzania or perhaps the long trailing shoulder of Mozambique. We had left Dar es Salaam some days before, which was always a quietening experience. Leaving Dar always meant a long journey ahead, but mostly it was because I loved the city. I loved it simply because of its name, no other reason. Dar es Salaam: the house of peace. All cities should be named for a virtue or a state of being, not for posturing men of a forgotten time or names buried in the debris and rubble of history. Refuge of the Wise. Kingdom of the Kind. House of Peace. I loved the vision and the hope, the ideal.

Sharma surveyed the length of the coast with his telescope. We were now closer to the shore, but I was unsure what, if anything, new could be seen through the glass. The air was hazy with heat. The blue of the sky and the sea was covered by a wash of mist. Clarity was not possible. There was nothing sharp on which to focus.

Lowering the telescope and returning it to its case, Sharma cleared his throat, but said nothing. He continued with his duties on the bridge for some time. His duties chiefly demanded only his presence. There wasn't much doing. The ship and crew were perfectly capable of navigating and maintaining a course on their own. Sharma's presence simply kept everyone's attention on their work and quiet conversation to the job at hand.

My duties were even simpler: to clean up after Sharma.

After he left, I retraced his steps, collecting his personal objects, replacing others to their rightful spots. I closed journals, re-shelved charts, re-capped pens. I picked up his mug to be returned to the ship's mess. I retrieved his eyeglasses, always left behind, and went to collect his telescope as well.

This time, the case was where he had left it, but it was empty. Usually easy to spot, the copper and brass of the telescope was nowhere to be seen. Among the white metal and whiter linoleum, it should have been clearly visible. The blue ribbon used to secure it in its nesting spot in the case was loose and untied.

What was I to think? Moses had been there, in the very room, doing what, I was uncertain. Everyone else had been seated, attending to their jobs or watching the radar, sonar, radio and other instruments, heads down and busy. The captain and I had been standing mostly near the starboard windows watching the distant African coast. I suppose Sharma could have taken the telescope with him, collapsing it partially into his broad pocket, but I did remember seeing him putting it back in the case. I could even imagine seeing him neatly retying the ribbon with a bow at each end.

Moses was my suspect. Sharma was the one to verify my suspicions.

Without knowing what would happen next, I found him. He was still on his way to his cabin, moving slowly, talking to those that he met. "Captain, Captain Sharma," I called. My voice was more urgent than I intended. The tea mug was still in my hand. The empty spyglass box was in the other. I waved it as I spoke. "Your telescope, do you have your telescope?"

He looked back at me. "No. It's not with you, Vishesh?"

"No. The box is empty." Holding the latch, I let it fall open so he could see inside.

"Let it be, Vishesh."

I couldn't believe my ears. "It's stolen," I protested.

"It's only a telescope." The captain was looking at something out on the water. "It's not vital. A toy really, just a device for peering and tinkering. A tube with glass, optics."

I wasn't understanding completely. A crime had been committed. A wrong needed to be righted. I looked at the captain.

"Give me the box," he said. He spoke kindly.

Together we walked the decks and interior quarters, even the engine room, asking until we found Moses. With other deckhands, he was stationed near the stern of the ship, tending to the maintenance of some grillwork.

"Moseby," the captain called. "You will need the box to keep the scope from the sea air. Corrosion. It's a problem with all these things. Metal devices, if they haven't been treated, seize up, useless." Sharma held the box before him. "I should have given you the box as well," he said. "My failing there. Forgive me."

Moses looked confused. He was uncertain what to say, which direction to take the conversation. "Sir?" he said, half question, half agreement.

"The telescope is my gift to you," Sharma explained, "but it won't last long without the protection of the box, not long at all. A bit of cleaning might be need as well. Lemon will do it."

Moses pulled the telescope from the rag bag hooked over his shoulder. He placed it carefully in the box, at first getting it in the wrong direction. Reversing, he tied both pairs of ribbons and shut the lid, securing the latch.

"Sir," he said. With sharp formality, he handed the box back to the captain.

"Perhaps," Sharma said, "we can let the boy look after it for us. For the time being." He passed the box onto me. "Vishesh is good with lost things."

We turned to leave. I stared at the boxed telescope now in my hands. I read the embossed inscription on the lid: Cumberland & Sons.

Sharma was still facing Moses, not quite finished. "Maybe you can be kind enough to instruct Vishesh in the proper use of the instrument, Moseby. When you have time. I would much appreciate that. If you are going to do something, it is worth doing it right," he said.

Both Moses and I were silent.

"As you were," the captain added.

Sharma had a way of solving problems by never actually addressing them directly. Some might feel he avoided confrontation, eluded the necessary. From what I saw, it was always something more: an act of kindness.

Looking back, the incident with Moses and the telescope was an unusual bit of business. It was a chapter that opened and closed, but didn't fundamentally change anything. At best, Sharma's solution probably avoided bigger problems down the line, but it also raised us out of the mundane for a time.

Soon, however, everything was back to normal – an undistinguished flow of sameness, each day much like the one that preceded it. If change is what you need, do not board a ship crossing an ocean. The change will be a long time coming. And then it will be sudden.

My description of football and gambling might make it sound like it was sports day every day, a casino hall of chance with Lady Luck on call, but it was far from that. At sea, there is a lot of sameness to endure. There is a lot of in-between – in between leaving and arriving, in between getting up and going to bed, in between one meal and the next.

Sameness is the hallmark of the sea. At first it is a tedium, endured, tolerated, finally embraced. It is endured because there is no choice. It is tolerated because mild or extreme insanity are the only alternatives. Finally, it is embraced because the understanding comes: the only change is the weather and that kind of stormy, violent pitching brings with it strain – both to the ship and to the crew. It also creates a new awareness of the lifeboats, swinging in their stations beckoning for passengers with every sway. But then, as the sailors say, the weather is a cool bluffer. More likely than not, everything returns to what it was. Call the weather's bluff and normalcy is restored. Tedium returns. Now she is an honoured guest.

At sea, the only satisfying change that can be truly welcomed is that glorious threesome – a port, a dockside berth and shore leave. And those are all usually a long way off, beyond the horizon, dreams on a map – the wonder of signal lights, crosswalks, restaurant menus, stairs that are not ladders. The list goes on.

Be clear: a freighter is not an ocean liner. Do not confuse the two. There is no dance floor or captain's table, no promenade deck, no activities officer, shuffleboard or burgeoning buffet offering food as entertainment. Time on an ocean liner is marked by meals separated by leisurely strolls and shaded naps. On a freighter there are only two sets of numbers: days-out-of-port, eventually replaced by days-until-arrival. Hatched lines – one, two, three, four, the fifth a sash tying the first four together.

The cruise ships are dreamliners, hotels-upon-the-sea, with names like Princess and Majesty, Allure, Oasis and Fantasy. Our freighter was the *Marathi Pride*, Marathi being about the only language not spoken by the multi-lingual crew. The pride also might have been false. It came mostly because we'd made it this far in our patched and rusted box pushing against the water. The *Marathi Pride* was a grey lady in whom we entrusted our lives. For that, we respected her. Our pride was blended with an equal measure of caution.

There were sometimes things to see when the *Pride* was skirting a shoreline or passing an island: a wisp of rising smoke, a line of colour, a sharp reflecting light from a window perhaps, the flickering movement of a real life among the trees and foliage. This was a favourite amusement, an entertainment for me. With the Cumberland telescope, premium navy-issue binoculars or the unaided eye, we all, Captain Sharma included, focused attention on anything that was not water. We might as well have been in an orbiting spacecraft for all that we could reach out and actually touch any humans in their distant and mirage-like settlements.

It was a lonely life. If we had actually been able to see a smiling face would we have felt better?

But then there were the birds. They followed the ship, drawn to us, yearning for a perch or a scrap of food, as much as we hoped for a walk in a forest or a green stretch of grass. The birds – I counted them, recorded their attendance, measured their length of stay. Unlike us, God had gifted them with wings, a means of departure and escape.

There are so many limitations on a ship, such a precision of choices. It is like being in a hammock all the time. You are subject to the sway and motion of the sea, but without any control. In both situations, you are contained and restricted. Sleep is an option, but nothing has changed when you awake. What you have, you have. Nothing can be imported, brought onboard, added to the limited inventory. Like a hammock, the effort to get out is too much. Sleep is the only escape, a temporary solution.

As a young man – a boy really in the eyes of the others – under the wing of Captain Sharma, I was spared the soul-confining drudgery that was the reality of life for the rest of the crew: painting, repainting, painting again, scraping rust, patching, mending, maintaining. But what were we maintaining? It was simply a boat cargoing containers of invisible, anonymous contents from Bombay to Bangkok to Mogadishu to Mauritius. It was a shell game, but we never saw what was under the cup we were shuffling across the table. The shipping containers were mute and anonymous, their contents a mystery. I suppose Sharma knew. He had access to the ship's manifests, but those were only words on paper. In truth, the *Marathi Pride* was destined, like all of us, for only one final port of call. In her case, it would be a tidal flat on the Bay of Bengal at the hands of the Chittagong ship-breakers, unrepairable, uninsurable, only steel, no longer a ship, without a spirit, without a soul. What purpose is there in that?

Although I was excused from the painting and scraping by virtue of my special appointment, I might have been better off with a paint brush or wire-toothed pad. My tedium was of my own making. Long days, cycled one into another, that is my memory of the first months on the *Marathi Pride*. The sameness was a test. There was no space for cricket, no talk of batsmen and runs. There was no dusty roads scented by the smell of cattle or the call of the cowherds. There was no Sat to enter my days unannounced, no Patel to give me eggs in the morning, no ring of the chai bell to break the monotony of the afternoon. It was like my father's store, but without the customers, without the running, without the petty sales or the chai breaks. It was my father's store without my father: just work and waiting for work.

I wanted to be in a crow's nest, the first to cry, "Land ho!" at the sight of a new world. Instead, I was sewing buttons on shirts, threading and re-threading shoelaces until the length balanced, doing nothing but looking for something to do – something new.

That's what it was like – at first.

TELESCOPE

You might say that Sharma's spyglass was like a key to a treasury. Its placement into my care unlocked doors I had not known. But to be more precise, the Cumberland telescope was not exactly the key. It was the keyhole. Those doors could not be opened, only peeked through.

What a miracle these instruments must have been to the explorers who first used them to scan the horizon in search of new worlds, islands that might supply fresh water, trade, food or rest. Like a lab microscope that can reveal the hidden world of microbes, a good telescope can change a rough sketch into a finely detailed schemata. Details are enlarged. The invisible can be seen. And then, they turned those same instrument skyward: what wonders to behold!

Remember this: I was a newcomer to life at sea. I was unable to read the waves, blind to the language of currents and tides. To me, all the birds and fish had a sameness. To my eyes, they revealed nothing of approaching land or changing seasons. The skies, likewise, at first revealed nothing. Day in and day out, I was an illiterate when it came to observation. As one shipmate called me, I was Analfabeto. I was the one with no alphabet. I could decipher nothing.

Sharma was happy not to carry and care for the telescope. Deferring the jobs to me solved a problem. I suppose he thought he might look like a snooping pirate or an orchestra conductor swinging that telescope about, using it as a pointer or a battling sword. Or, simply, he might have feared that he might again leave it somewhere, forgotten on deck, ready to roll into the drink or a precious thing ready to fall prey to thieving hands. He was like that, both careless and cautious.

So whenever I had the chance, whenever there was something worth viewing, the scope was at the ready. I knew where that magic glass was at all times and Sharma had no problem with me popping it to my eye, to assess and report. He encouraged me. "Give the Cumberland glass a shot," he might say. The telescope was both our scout and our spy.

Passing ships, floating debris, islands and coastlines were prime. Birds and jumping fish were of interest, but their quick movements and fleeting appearance made them a poor match for my slow movements and even slower focussing.

The optics and focal length of the spyglass, I first thought, made this particular telescope best suited for lunar observations. Through it, the moon was a brilliant orb with detailed mountains and shadow-filled valleys. Both the wax and wane became a spectacular show. From a flat disc of light to a ball, circular, hanging and orbiting across the dark sky, the moon came alive through the scrutiny of that telescope.

The glass, however, had little effect on the stars, only making them smaller and sharper. It robbed them of their twinkle. They became pinpoints holes pricked out of the blackness, not distant suns of fire.

Nonetheless, the telescope brought the heavens to my attention. Both the moon and the stars had a beauty that I loved, but still also something of a sameness that was predictable. It was life on land that was the real subject for intense viewing. Human life is not set in predictable orbits and in that lies the chance for real discovery.

I held the glass to my eye and slid the outer section forward. The image zoomed in slightly. What had been an island floating on an ocean became a forest and beach. Four parallel bands of colour, from top to bottom: blue sky, green trees, white sand, blue water.

As I panned left to right, it was like the stripes of a flag. The colours were unbroken, waving slightly in the breeze, but solid and constant as my eye moved down the long coast.

I tried again, a bit closer. I steadied the image by propping my elbows on the railing, anchoring my feet a little farther apart into a solid, secure stance. Still, the motion of the ship made it difficult, the slight up and down as we rode the waves. I tried again, to stabilize, to compensate. There now: something for sure, some colour and movement in two directions at the same time. What was it?

I wiped the lens with the clean end of a handkerchief. I re-focused the spyglass with care and precision. Something was there, but not with the clarity I wanted. If only the ship was closer. I looked up at the bridge, willing them to change course, circle the island please, closer on a second pass. That would be unlikely. Detours cost money and shallow waters are always to be avoided.

I tried again. Focussing and squinting, my hand felt along the neck: zoom ring, focus ring and then another ring of metal. This one was flat and polished. Unlike the others, it was not grooved with lines for grip.

I rotated the wheel. The image zoomed and focused simultaneously, sharp and clear. I felt again along the barrel of the telescope. I pressed a small recessed button. Like dropping a filter over the image, it darkened. The contrast improved. I was seeing like never before.

There before me was a beach with people. They looked Chinese or perhaps Malaysian. I could see that close – both faces and eyes.

But then there were others as well. I could not see everything at once. Slowly my brain gathered the elements of the image, slowly processing, understanding. Not just Chinese, others: some Indian, some European, Africans. From every nation, these people, some walking, some standing at the edge of the water. Some with their feet in the warm coral sea. I strained to see closer, to hear their voices, to be with them.

On the shore of a great ocean, all the people of the world together. One man on the flat of the beach where the dry white sand changed to the wet black of the ocean. I could not see his face or his nationhood. It was obscured by a set of black binoculars. He was looking directly at me.

Could they also see the ship, the *Marathi Pride* chugging? Could this man see me looking at him?

He raised his right arm full and straight. Slowly he waved left to right in a broad motion. Slowly he waved at me across the waters, beckoning, calling me to join.

I raised my own arm, reserved and furtive. And then I withdrew.

I thought about that man quite a bit. What was he doing, waiting at the water's edge – honouring the sea, preparing for my arrival or, simply, being there with all the others?

That man entered into my dreams, his face still indistinct, shadowed or blurred or else a composite of many faces at once. I spoke to him and he replied with a grace and a wisdom. He knew me, even if I did not know him. He listened to me. Even as he spoke, he listened. But when I awoke, the world of the dream evaporating with the morning light, I could not remember his words. Still, his presence lingered.

I tried to imagine the place he lived. The people who gathered with him on that beach. Were they always there? Did they assemble just to see us pass, so distant, a mirage on the heat-waved horizon?

Then I questioned what I had seen, whether it was so. Was it a confusion caused by too much sun, by not enough water, by a desire unresolved? When I inspected the telescope, I could never quite get it to function in the same manner. The focus ring and zoom seemed loose to my touch. The precision was lost. The third ring and recessed button seemed dirtied, infested by sand or grit. I fiddled with the mechanisms, their combination and relation to each other. Every time, when I felt I almost had it, I would be interrupted, called for a task or asked a question. When I returned to the scope, it was like starting over.

Soon I gave up. But I did not give up remembering and imagining.

STARS

I am lying in my hammock. It is hot. I am outside. There are a thousand thousand stars. There is no sway to my hammock. There is is no movement on the ocean. Is the ship dead, drifting and rudderless, or is time at a standstill?

Am I asleep? How long have I been awake?

There is a stillness. There is no movement, no time.

I am remembering something. It is now. This is the moment I am recalling. I have been here before. Many times.

A thousand thousand stars, pinholes, salt and dust, but not just sprinkled and scattered. These stars reach back. There is depth. I am not looking at a ceiling spray-painted with light like a planetarium projection. I am not inside looking at the edges. I am not in a seat watching the stage. I am. That is all. It goes on and on. The stars are only the beginning. How long have I been awake or am I just now awakening? For the first time.

If this was a ship of sail, we would be becalmed. I hear the water gently lapping on the ship's side. I am remembering a beach. A silent rain. A fragrant wind. A woman at the centre. But it is not the beach, the rain or the woman alone. It is the feeling: a unity, complete. I want that again and not just for a moment. For always.

The stars stretch on forever, in all directions, back and back, towards and inside. There are a multitude. Then there is only one.

Am I awake? How long have I been awake I cannot measure.

NAVIGATION

Sharma told me that the stars can be used for navigation.

"At sea, the stars are the only constant," he said starting from nowhere, in answer to no question. "They seem to move across the sky, but we are the ones moving. The North Star steady and constant. All others circle that star." His fist rotated in the air between us, a small Earth in the vast universe of the ship's bridge.

"Now we use satellites and radios, charts and maps. Global positioning systems have changed everything. It is easier, but the same. We want to know where we are. The oceans are covered with lines, shipping lanes, express routes for ships like us. All we have to do is look for the correct exit."

He smiled in the small way he had, more trying to suppress the smile than to encourage it, pleased at his own wisdom, but at the same time afraid of the bigger questions.

"The stars are a good way to navigate. They served Magellan and Marco Polo, all of them." He laughed to himself again. Sometimes when he spoke to me, it was as if he was talking to himself. He never looked at me when he made the words, only when he was listening. "All of them – that is what the word means. Universe – everything is one, unified. So we do know where we are after all." He let his fist rotate and open to a flat palm. "We are here. In the universe."

•

The captain taught me navigation – the old and new ways, both. He had me calculate and recalculate our course, plot it on a map, estimate the days and hours to our next port arrival and then compare my results to the ship's GPS and the estimates and reckonings of the ship's navigator. It was a game.

He gave me an empty merchant navy ledger, a broad columned book with great decorative anchors and handled helm wheels. I created my own log of the ship's journeys and voyage. The journeys were between the ports. Together they added up to the final voyage either to the ship-breaking yards or to some heaven, a nirvana for sainted ships. I ignored the anchors and wheels. The anchors stop you from moving. The wheels only take you across the face of the compass, only on the flatness of the water. I wanted to go farther.

In my log, with time and imagination, I created new columns: date, time, weather conditions, of course. Then crew and duties according to my observations and expectations. Moving to the right, across the double, facing pages, I entered columns for birdlife observed (species, number, direction, comments), fish observed, waves and currents, stories told by crew, noted by type (sad stories, jokes, exaggerations, lies, hopes and plans). In another column I recorded meals (real and imagined). The final, and most important, columns were for thoughts and dreams and all imaginary lands passed. Footnotes gave the coordinates, longitudes and latitudes of each of these places. Numbered codes linked to a second book. This second volume was filled with secret accounts of these lands. Detailed alongside were finely drawn maps and illustrations. It was a labour of love. Because there was life, creation and passion, it was effortless and time passed.

A box-shaped island was circumnavigated today. No visible port could be seen. The coasts were straight with no invitation to land, no sheltering harbours or river mouths. As we prepared to leave, a welcoming committee in out-rigger longboats approached and boarded our ship. They spoke English well enough, but could not pronounce some words. For other words, they had no knowledge or use. For things and ideas for which English had no label, they made their own fresh sounds and ingenious spellings. Their land is a principality governed by a benevolent king, a giant, a man-mountain they call Uncle or Father or more often He. They avoid his name. There is no currency or exchange medium. Their commerce is based on gift-giving. They call their land Galbony and hope that we will return soon. They gave each of us small hand-woven pockets filled with scented sea salts. Their smiles will not be easy to forget.

Today we caught sight of a phantom ship passing at seven leagues NNE. The speed could not be calculated because a firm focus could not be attained. It drifted and faded and then, without warning, would appear in another spot on a new track and heading. Its speed was remarkable. We tried to establish a communication link, but it seems to have been only in one direction. We could hear them, but they did not respond to us. Their calls continued unabated, unchanged by our words. "Beware, be cautious, continue, do not falter. Always be calm like the ocean." I have marked their position on the accompanying map and a projection of their route, but that is simple unguided speculation.

The Salaam Sea. In this area we sighted a federation of several island nations or city states. They are arranged alpha-numerically in a poorly defined ring or near-circle about twenty-five leagues across, each equidistant from a most beautiful central atoll of coral and walnut and scented jasmine. Each scent alone is a pure diluted concentrate. Together they are a jubilant masala. We had been anchored there for almost a fortnight, when we learned it was the time of Walna, an occasional gathering of thirty-seven nations in what is both an intellectual summit and cultural festival and celebration. This event is an open exchange of ideas and discoveries, free from discrimination, mistrust and competition. It is a time of truce and amnesty when all other activities are dropped in favour of forgiveness and acceptance. The favoured form of discourse is a long form prose-poem known as a "pleason." Our visit to the Salaam Sea resulted in a morale boast for the entire crew. Our dinner conversations are now much more spirited. Our health has improved.

In this way, I passed my time. No longer interested in what was not, I turned to what could be. My imagination flowed freely and without constraint. The ship was filled with everything it lacked. I stacked the shelves high with my dreams.

It had been like this: at first I had been interested in counting the days. But, as those days passed, I lost interest in both the days and in counting. What had been before was without benefit. Days are nothing. They are units, convenient measurements, another chance to take the bat, to take a wicket, to measure success and failure. Months, seasons, years: God gives us so many chances, opportunities to do better. And what do we do? – the same thing over and over.

So I lost count of the days, the nautical miles, the leagues, the temperature. I could not count the stars, so why count anything? Our ship moved from port to port in ever-widening circles. Seasons seemed to disappear as we moved from one hemisphere to the other. No more spring measured by fresh flowers. No monsoon season measured by rainfall. No more cricket season measured by the crowning of another championship team.

It might have been the changing face of the world: globalization, commerce and economics. Needs and wants, the fortunes of world trade, brought us to many new ports in many new countries. Some seemed like imaginary places plucked from the pages of my private logbook. Others seemed like retreads, the same cities under new names, a different arrangement of buildings and docks, but otherwise the same thing all over again.

Then one day it came from nowhere: I had enough. There was comfort on *Marathi Pride*. There was a family – of sorts. There was Captain Sharma and there was order. But I came to know that there was more for me beyond that ship. Goodbyes were not needed. I just wanted that thing that was more. I wanted to live in and walk the streets of one of those places in my logbook. I knew it was possible.

In the deadest moment of the night, when movement and thought and direction do not exist, when action and reason are not brothers, I abandoned my hammock. I took nothing with me. I had nothing to take. Our ship was moored in what seemed to be the outer harbour of an unnamed city – I hadn't paid attention to learn the name. Confidently, but without the comfort of any knowledge or bearings, I stepped down the temporary scaffolding steps on the side of the ship. I boarded the small skiff loosely tied there by a returned shore leave crew.

Silent, without motor or paddle, I gently pushed off. Under the white light of an almost full moon, I drifted on that empty harbour, the city unseen. I could have been anywhere. There once had been a time when I would have known the longitude and latitude, the minutes and seconds, my exact position on the globe's graph paper surface. I had lost count because I did not care.

I lay in that small boat, my legs under one of the bench seats. I looked at the stars, a beautiful oneness. Not interested in counting, instead I numbered my breaths: one and one and one.

Now I was sleeping, but totally aware in my unknown surroundings.

SHARMA SPEAKS

I am the captain of a freighter. As the years have gone by, the value of that ship seems to have diminished like so much water evaporating in the heat of the sun. A ship that goes back and forth carrying the same cargo, year after year, that takes men nowhere is not a ship of substance. There is no purpose, no satisfaction. It is only a time machine – a machine that is a waste of time. It takes men into the future of their own lives, avoiding what others easily accept, that life means family and friends and the flow of human contact. The sea is a void and life there is a life without.

I boarded this ship as a young man. I had a crisp shirt and a crisper salute. Look at me now. I am old and the ship has rusted and aged as well. Men do not grow young. That is our curse, I feel. No one grows young unless they are blessed by an alert mind and an optimistic outlook.

Why I am here, I can barely remember now. It was not so much a decision, as a course laid out for me by my father and his father. It seemed obvious to them, to everyone. My father had been in the navy himself and had some distinction and privilege. Status might be a better way to describe it. His brothers, my uncles, were the same – career sailors, servants of the sea, officers of bearing. You are born into a family and that is that. They set your course and push off, on your way.

It was a course without headwinds. And I did not resist. If anything, I rose to the occasion, played the part to the full. My aim was to please – to please my father first, then to please the shipping corporation. Now I try to please the crew. I pity them.

For me, the result has been a suffering for myself and my own family. While other men might say, "I will be a little late for dinner tonight," I would say, "I will see you in three months when I return." Three months, six months, a year, what is the difference? Do I really know my children? They grow so fast. Do I know my wife or only the memory of the shy girl I married so long ago? And now there are grandchildren – strangers to me as well.

Maybe this is why I asked that boy to join us in Bombay. I miss the company of someone I can call family, someone to teach and pass on whatever I have. Meanings harvested over the years are small, but do need to be shared.

Vishesh was sharp. He learned fast. He knew what I needed before I did. But then, after a time, I began to think what world did I bring him to?

The merchant navy seemed once to be a clear cut choice – crisp like the salutes, smart like the collars, fresh air, fulfilling a duty, supplying the needs of life to the people of the world, a vital service to the nation.

But service is not everything. The horizon is never reached. It calls and recedes. It beckons, but you are never there.

I could see that the boy was smarter than me. It didn't take long. The tedium of the ship was getting to him years before it even hinted at the underpinnings of my own life. The limits, the routine, the mindless repetition is a rust that eats away at a man, undetected, unseen. It takes a toll. You do not know what you are missing, how your life is not as full as it might have been on shore. You never know that you are in discomfort until you experience that which others call normal. Luxury would be torture.

What if I had stayed in Goa? What if I had tended a tea shop on the beach? Would I have enjoyed the sunsets more if in the company of customers and friends rather than from the bridge of this ship and a salaried crew of misfits? There are no what-if worlds, only the one you have been living. The idea of parallel lives is the fantasy of a fool.

I set tasks for Vishesh, anything to keep him happy or entertained. I taught him the basics of navigation. I told him our next port of call and had him set a course. I taught him how to read the sky, the stars and the weather. I taught him both the science and the lore of the sea. Still, his tedium grew. Numbers and charts and calculations were only a short term solution.

I could see when he lay in his hammock that his tedium grew even as he slept. His dreams were those of places greater, rich in wonders, eternal with their rewards.

What is the use of navigation? To predict a course and then follow it only makes a life into a clockwork. There is no surprise. If outcome successfully matches prediction, then you are asked to do it all again.

The imagination can be a place of fear and terror. It can also be a land of miracles. I said small things at first. "Vishesh, what if there was a land between us and Jakarta that was hostile with pirates and phantoms, how would you navigate those waters?" "What if there was a sea called Doubt and another dubbed Peace?" "What if a volcano rose from the ocean floor with a lava that flowed with wisdom?" "What if our cargo was courage? What if we traded in innocence and faith? What if the pole star was love and all our navigation was a calculation from that point? What course would you choose from that? What would be your bearing, your true line? What sort of compass would you design to get us across those seas?"

I had never spoken to anyone like that. Perhaps what-if worlds do exist if we wish, if we give our permission, if we desire with a wholeness fully summoned. It is not money that buys happiness. It is desire. Maybe we are the sparks who will kindle a new life for those who follow.

The Pacific is a big ocean. It is the largest. Sometimes the name is quite suited to its nature. Other times it is a grey solitude of hopelessness. From Taipei to Seoul and then across the North Pacific can test a man. At my age I do not want tests any more. I fear I will no longer pass.

I feel I am receding from life, no longer an active player, no longer a star, now a second choice, something from the past.

I feel I have moved from the stage to the audience. I know I am in a play, a farce quite often. It is the third act. The bar in the lobby beckons. In life there are no interludes. It just goes on and on.

I took Vishesh aside. "When we make our next port, take your chance," I said. "It will be a place as good as any. There is nothing to go back to. Move forward and find your way. There is an affluence there that draws many, but that is not for you. It is a new land and that can mean a lot – opportunity, fewer rules, fewer men like me to tell you how and when."

Vishesh looked at me with an understanding that few can manage. His eyes widened with clarity. His demeanor was caring. He was beyond his years, an old soul if ever there was one.

"Take my compass," I said. "But do not believe it. It only knows one thing. North is just one way. The world has a multitude of directions. Don't take it as a souvenir, a memory of me. You will meet many others better. I am just one. Take the compass as a key you can pass on to them. Endow it with your own wisdom, not just the knowledge of north.

"Change the world, Vishesh."

I didn't know if I had said too much. Maybe sending him off into a strange land was wrong. I knew he did not want to be with us on the *Pride* any more. I knew that I had given him all that I could give. But mostly and most truly, I knew that I was asking him to do what I dearly wanted to do myself had I the legs, the youth, the spirit and the optimism.

I was giving him permission to jump ship.

"It would please me very much if you would take this," I said, handing him the old compass.

"Thank you, uncle," Vishesh nodded. He had never called me uncle until that day. Captain is a term of respect imposed to keep order and discipline. Uncle is a term of both respect and love. It connects us. It does not divide.

we were in a temple

Trees are the Earth's endless effort
to speak to the listening heaven.

Rabindranath Tagore

NEW LAND

It is the cowdust time. Morning. I walk the quiet street. I must seem like an alien, red shirt, brown skin, thin, wiry, unaccustomed to the gravity in this new world.

This is not a city. It is a large port with a small town attached. With each step I am changing – a boy, an Indian, a sharpener of pencils, a scorekeeper, a runner, an explorer, a sailor, a navigator, a reader of maps, a map-maker – each step is uncharted. This new land is silent and still. I breathe deeply. Sea salt and fish, seaweed and wet wood, cedar and hemlock mixed. I know this place, this new world. It is like my own, rich with smells.

It is summer. There is a warmth even though it is still early. It is warmth unfamiliar to this land, the slow baking of that which has been months wet. I walk and walk. I take in everything. At first no people. A black, black bird caws at me, laughs, warns and laughs again. It is threatening. It will only give me one chance.

Then people: a distant car or two. A woman opening a kitchen curtain. An idling taxi. Traffic lights, red, but no one to stop. A seagull pulling at a torn paper bag. A man, his car stacked high with newspapers tosses the folded news to doorsteps and shop doors. After he leaves, I take one. It has landed in a garden bush. It is for me.

I walk on. Taking in everything: oil and lube, tire rotation, free upgrade, visitors bureau, tourist information, no parking, street cleaning Tuesdays, chamber of commerce, no stopping.

A man is approaching on the sidewalk. I hold my newspaper tightly, hitting it against my leg nervously. He does not look at me. He is bearded, worn-eyed, foreign – foreign to me. Where is he going so early or is he returning to his home? He is looking down, studying the path he will take. Then, at the last moment: eye contact. "Morning," he says. He turns and crosses the empty street. He walks towards a hotel. Regal. Gentlemen's Entrance. Nitely.

"Good morning," I reply. He is gone.

I continue on, down the street. I can smell sweet warm bread, but I cannot see it. Will anyone be selling eggs? I stop. An orange hand tells me to wait. The light, now a white man walking, tells me to proceed. The road is empty. It is called Third.

A seagull, a familiar call. I follow his voice. Second Street. First Street. This town has a pleasing simplicity, a predictability and order. When the street counting stops, I am again at the ocean, a calm lapping, not rolling and wave–driven. The mountains are low and enormous at the same time, blue in the morning light.

I take the newspaper. It is now my pillow. I lie on the small beach. The sand is cold, wet, but drying slowly. Lines of seaweed are sketched along the shore. I rest. I feel I have been deposited by the high tide. "Maybe Sat will find me," I think as I close my eyes. I am not alone.

SURRENDER

I only slept a short time. After so long at sea, it was strange to be on unmoving land. I was used to the swaying hammock. It had surely been one of our longest voyages and, after the crossing of the Pacific, was I feeling a little landsick?

I was somewhere new. And it was also a fresh start. I wasn't afraid, but I wanted to do it right. I wasn't sure how.

Walking the street, I saw something that brought back memories. It was a shop, very different, but also very much the same as my father's. This store sold fruits and vegetables. Was there a running boy, another version of myself waiting inside. I looked at the shops, so far apart. Running here would be much farther, but still easier. There was not the heat, not the traffic, no crowds of people.

I was hungry, but I had another idea as well. I had some money, three American bills. Maybe they would work.

I selected one banana, one apple and, with great care to make the best choice, a coconut. I took them inside and placed them on the cashier's counter. I did not speak. The woman weighed and totalled the purchase. The cash register read $1.89. I offered her two American one dollar bills. She looked at the money and then at me. "At par," she said, taking the banknotes.

I was not certain what that meant. It sounded like Hindi, but wasn't. I had my fruits and also now two coins, one small and silver, the other copper. On the street, I looked at them. The silver one had a picture of a boat, beautiful with a broad sail. The other coin was decorated with leaves from a tree of some kind. This seemed good – the sea and the land. The back of both coins were the same: a woman in profile and the words "ELIZABETH II – D. G. REGINA." The woman seemed to be wearing a small crown. In the sky above the boat and on the other coin below the leaves was the same word: CANADA.

This was Canada. There was a queen and a kingdom. They liked boats and trees. They took American money "at par." This was America, but another America. There was a lot to learn.

I put the coins in my pocket. I carried the apple, banana and coconut in the white plastic bag I had been given. I saw a tree with leaves similar to the ones pictured on the copper coin. I took four and added them to my bag.

I walked along the coast, out of the town and higher onto the rocks overlooking the ocean. I had not gone far. The town was small or maybe I was just at the edge. I sat, silent within myself. "This is all new," I felt. "I want to be new also."

I remembered Nargol and Patel and the temple. I placed the four leaves on the rockface. Each leaf pointed in a different direction like a compass. I put Sharma's compass at the centre, rotating it until the N aligned with the pointing needle. I took the banana out of the bag.

"I offer this fruit from India, the food of that land." I bowed my head to feel the words and their meaning.

I took the apple with the same dedication. "I offer this fruit of this land, this Canada. Make my time here without obstacle."

The coconut was next. I wasn't sure what to say. The coconut is auspicious, but I wasn't sure of the right words. They put coconuts at the temple gate, I remembered. It was always at the pujas and weddings. I took the coconut in both hands. I could feel the water moving inside. "From all the oceans," I said, "the water from all the oceans of the world, from all the rivers, I offer to you." I put the coconut between four small stones to keep it from rolling. "It would make me happy if you can accept," I added.

I took the two coins from my pocket and placed them in front of the coconut. "Bless this land and all who walks on her. Forgive us if our tread is too heavy or we make mistakes. Keep me steady and clear."

I remembered Patel. I placed the flat palms of both of my hands on the smooth rock. It felt cool and calming. I bowed my head until it also touched the cold stone. "I surrender to you."

I remembered Patel's words, "Surrender is not giving up, it is worship."

"Show me how to step," I said, "so that it pleases you. Make me one with you and also this land. Be with me."

I sat up and was silent for some time.

I ate the banana and apple and placed the coconut gently in the ocean and watched it drift away.

I put the compass in my shirt pocket near my heart.

RUPERT

The town was called Prince Rupert. I saw the name throughout the pages of my newspaper. Prince Rupert, a principality without a castle or a live-in monarch it seemed. I surveyed this landfall, a natural deep seaport, protected and safe on the edge of the world's biggest ocean. Coal and timber and grain terminals lined the channel harbour. Container ships, like the *Marathi Pride*, unloaded and restocked. I could see the Marathi now, dockside. I hid myself, laid low until she silently departed. I was not saddened, although I thought of Sharma. He had told me to leave, words I wanted to hear, but I wished now he had come with me. I also knew that our time together had finished, completed and closed.

Prince Rupert was a small town. Sixteen thousand people the signboard read. Where were they all? This was definitely not an India, teeming with onlooker, shoppers and spectators. This was Canada, not Karnataka. In India, it seemed to take at least half a dozen clerks and apprentices and managers and boys to complete any transaction – paperwork in triplicate – plus a few onlookers and idle commentators or naysayers. Everything in this Rupert seemed self-serve, open for business, free-form and new. It didn't need to be welcoming. It was frontier. Maybe everyone was new. At least there was no temple brahmin to tell you ten thousand years of tradition and the way to do it. I don't think there was even a temple.

Princely or not, Rupert was for me.

RUSTY

Without money and without friends, alone in a foreign land, I didn't know what to do next. I had my English, the same language as the people of Rupert if the shop signs and newspaper were an indication. And I had one other thing: a compass. Captain Sharma's silver pocket compass, the one he had given me, was still in my pocket. I turned it over slowly in my hand. It was dented with age, like the captain, but also bright and simple. I looked at it as I walked. As I turned direction, it pointed north, always, without doubt.

I followed the shore northward, as best as I could, following both the high tide line and the arm of the compass. Perhaps there was something to be found, something else forgotten and waiting, offered up by the sea. I thought of Sat. He would make something on the spot – some fishing line, a plastic bottle, a knot of rope and Sharma's shiny compass. Together they would find my way out of this mess.

It was past nine o'clock and only now starting to get dark. If there were cows and cowherds here in Rupert, they would already been home in stable and bed. I looked around. Nothing. No trails. No dust. No cow bells or calling herders.

The water of the inlet was calm. "How can an ocean be so calm and smooth?" I thought. The crashing waves of the Arabian Sea were far away. Here the water was calm, a darkening blue, rich with co-lour. The water, the mountained islands and the sky were joining into one as the night gathered. I remembered my mother. "This is the time the Earth does yoga." Her words added comfort.

There was a ripple, a turning and a splash. I squinted. Not a fish, but more like a dog, gone and back again.

"A harbour seal," someone whispered.

I looked. There was a man, young, maybe about my age. It was hard to tell. He was my height, but with more flesh and fat. He was standing on a log, looking beyond me, towards the ocean. "They are after the fish," he said.

"That would be nice, a little food." I was hungry

He saw the compass, still in my hand. "Looking for something?" he asked.

"First time I've been here," I explained.

"All of us," he said, whispering again, confiding.

There are different varieties of people. Some talk with no end and say nothing. They just want to fill the airwaves, no dead air, no gaps, no silence.

Another type of person is always joking and it is always a variation of the same joke, without insight or reason. There is no freshness. It is a cycle of sound. It is a mask and a kind of a hiding.

There are those who speak only when spoken to. It is a guarded conversation, always on the surface. Nothing is given away. It is factual and empty.

There are people who consider everything and take in all ideas. The doors are open. The invitation is universal. The net is cast wide. Some may feel these people have no discretion, they are foolish or naive. Others take them to be progressive. Sometimes they are both.

There are people who speak only of things – what they will buy, what others own. Their conversation sounds like a catalogue, objects and service, discounts and special offers, but really it is all about desire, needs, wants and cravings. It is empty.

Then you may meet a man or a woman who talks only of people. At first, it sounds like concern, even love, but then you realize it is mostly gossip. "Did you hear? Did you know?" These people are most interested in the failings of others, the mistakes, the scandals. They want to show how they know better.

Still others again live in a world of ideas. Their words are wrapped in theories and concepts. They generalize and rarify. There are no things or people, only forces. These talkers are trend-spotters and futurists, theoreticians. They sound erudite and educated. They are often paid very well for the way they sound.

And then there are people who do not crave or gossip or preach. These people speak to the moment they are in. They do not restrict their thoughts and words to either things or people or ideas. They are not bounded by either the next moment or the one that just happened. They are in the present.

I think this man who stood before me on the beach in Prince Rupert was such a person. He didn't seem concerned about where I came from or where I was going. He was there and I was there. That is all that mattered.

"My name is Russell." He extended his hand in agreement and welcome.

"Mr. Russell," I repeated.

"Call me Rusty."

As I met his hand with mine, he grasped it in a double-fisted handshake. His handshake was firm and strong, but also friendly. He was not making a deal. He was making a promise. His welcome was genuine.

•

Rusty told me about Prince Rupert in a way a person does who is proud of their hometown. Facts were served with love, with delight and wonder. This deep and naturally protected harbour was a port for both global freighters and local fishermen. The place had been the dream of a railway man named Charles Hays. Maybe he was the real prince.

We talked into the darkness of the night. "Hays wanted this to be a place for cruise ships and tourists and lovers of mountains and glaciers," Rusty explained. "He loved the natural splendour and wanted to share it. This was his dream and he dreamt it a long time ago – about 1910. Then one of those glaciers, way in another ocean, got him. It sent out a chunk of ice and down he went inside the Titanic."

Rusty explained that this little town with a few thousand people, a village really by Indian standards, was actually one of the busiest ports in the country. I looked around. Maybe this was a slow day. Or maybe it was a small country. "Montreal and Halifax on one side," Rusty counted on his fingers, "then Vancouver and Rupert on this side. Fifteen or sixteen thousand people, everything just passes through onto the trains or trucks. Nothing for us except some jobs." It was the railway that opened Rupert to the continent. The road was pushed through later, a wartime defense against the Japanese.

"And, oh yeah, Hay's cruise ships are here now in the summer." Rusty pointed down the rocky shore to the whiteness of an enormous multi-floored ocean liner, pushing out into the water, now clearly visible lit in by row after row of windows. "The water is deep."

Rusty told me about his family, mostly fishermen and mechanics. He had both brothers and sisters, two of each like me. He liked to read about the world, but had no desire to travel. "Everything is here. Or comes here eventually," he offered in explanation. "Like you," he added with a laugh.

Towards the end he said everything about that place and himself in a few simple words: "Vishesh, I am Haida. I am this place."

"Haida?" I asked.

"First Nation. Indian."

"Indian," I understood. "Me too."

ANGELS

In school they taught us about guardian angels. God is a busy guy, they more or less said. He can't hear all the prayers that are sent his way. The smart Christian should also pray to a few saints. Going travelling, pray to Christopher. Lost something, Anthony will help. Or maybe your namesake is a good route to take – if your name is George, Saint George will look after you if he isn't too busy with dragons and such. A sure bet is to send a prayer to the Virgin Mary – another tip they told us. I suppose the thinking was that Jesus will always listen to his mother and she has the time to listen to you.

All this is not much different than Indians asking Shri Ganesha to remove the obstacles, Hanuman to quicken the journey or Shri Lakshmi to loosen the purse strings. There are different department for different kinds of requests.

Heaven is a busy place – so many Christians with so much to talk about – so many problems offered, so many solutions needed. If you've got a problem, you don't want to always get a busy signal or to be put on hold. "All our representatives are busy right now, we will be with you as soon as we can." So they had a good solution to deal with this backlog: guardian angels. Each person, every God-loving Christian boy and girl, had their own personalized angel, a guardian to monitor the situation daily, hourly if need be, on call, on the watch, making sure the road was smooth, no pitfalls, no pot-holes, ready to change a tire or redirect traffic.

I don't think I had a guardian angel. It's more likely I had many. There were a series of people who took me into their care, under their wings of protection. They guided me until it was time for me to move on. My mother was the first. She introduced me to this strange world. She held my hand and explained its workings. Patel and Sharma played their parts as well, with a gentle guiding wisdom. While my school teachers set limits, Sat showed me the tricks. If a teacher said, "Here is a fence," Sat showed me how to jump.

Rusty was now my new guardian. He saw in me both a friend and a brother. He watched out for me, showed me the ropes, as he called it. I decided that the best way to repay him was to look after for him as well. Angels also need help sometimes.

TOURISTS

As we had done on many mornings throughout that summer, Rusty and I stood on the dock not far from an Alaska-bound cruise ship. The people disembarking were looking for a change of pace – some local colour, a souvenir or two, a photograph next to a totem pole or maybe just some solid unmoving ground to stand on. Rusty was willing to supply any and all of these, plus some authentic cultural and stoic native wisdom.

Rusty's smile came easily. He was perfect for the job. From where did he come, a land of wonder, a childhood so totally blessed? Pleasure came to him easily. He simply enjoyed the one-big-joke of life and its continuous non-stop rollout. His smile was hard to dampen. It was his invitation to everyone: join me, see the world through my eyes.

In this way, Rusty was the ideal guide to Rupertland. And as for me, I stood by his side, his assistant, his partner, his fellow interpreter of the world. If he represented First Nationhood, I was New Nationhood, the immigrant from the world beyond the horizon. Together we were the new face of Canada – a tomorrowland of harmony and racial oneness. Perfect holiday viewing. The tourists loved it.

We called ourselves "Two Indians on a Bike." With a tandem two-seater bicycle attached to a rickshaw-style bench seat wagon, we pedaled up and down the flat streets of Prince Rupert. Rusty regaled the visitors with details of local history garnered mostly from leaflets he found in the public library, embroidered by his imagination. He did voices and dog barks, whistled like the wind and drew the northern lights with his fingers in the air.

"The town was named after Prince Rupert of the Rhine," he called back as we cycled. "Imagine an aristocratic 17th century Bavarian warrior. He was the royalest of royalist cavalier, like no other. He went into battle with his white poodle dog named Boye. The dog was a gift from his lover, Susie Kuffstein, who also happened to be the daughter of his jailer. Rupert was a prisoner of war – with a pet poodle. Imagine!

"But this Boye was no ordinary dog," Rusty explained to the slack-jawed tourists. "Boye was Rupert's familiar."

He took a long pause for dramatic effect. "The dog was his familiar," he repeated. "That means Boye was his animal guide, a trickster like the raven, sent to teach him the ways of the spirit world.

They were constant companions – Rup with Boye, Boye with Rup wherever you looked. Did I mention that some say that the poodle was actually a lady of Lapland transformed into the guise of a dog, better to assist Rupert in his witchly crafts?

"Boye, like I said, was a dog like no other, a rarity. Some said he could catch bullets in his teeth. He was invincible in battle. He could uncover hidden treasure. He was a sometime soothsayer, able to prophesy the future. If he wasn't actually prepared to catch the bullet, he could warn Rupert from which direction it would come.

"Anyways," Rusty tied up the tale neatly, "the people of this town liked that story so much, they had a contest. The first prize of $250 was awarded – that was a lot of money at that time – and the ideal name was chosen for their new digs. And so it was: Prince Rupert."

We pedaled around the town, got some snapshots at the totem poles, had a coffee and donuts and then ended up at the Rusty's souvenir stand. That's where I sold keychains, postcards and objects of art suitable for the mantel or the attic. A white poodle was tethered to fire hydrant, a touch of local colour. We didn't ask it to fetch any bullets.

Earlier on, Rusty confided to me, "I won't mention to them the part about dying on the Titanic. It's a bit of a downer for people travelling on a cruise ship." He laughed deeply. "Keep it simple. Not good for holiday morale."

RUSTY SPEAKS

My hair is not red. I do not move slowly or creak. I don't know why they call me Rusty. At first it was Russell. Then it was Russ. Those names were not me either. Russ – you'd expect a crewcut football-tosser with a name like that: Russ Jackson or Jack Russell, somebody like that.

Vishesh – I don't what that means. He fell from the sky or was washed up by the ocean. Do you know him? He's a special one, not set on conquering the world or rising to the top. He's like me that way – not a part of all this, just a tourist visiting this world from faraway, from an imaginary land to another imaginary land.

The first time I saw him I said there's a guy who maybe doesn't know what he wants, but is open to the possibilities. I like that. People with all the answers bore me. They have no vision, no fun. Everything is a calculated risk and the risk is usually calculated with dollar signs. They work for logging companies or the Port Authority. They're fine here, but really want to be in Vancouver or Toronto.

When I helped Vishesh figure out Canada, I wasn't really helping him. I was helping myself. Do you know what I mean? You think you are telling someone something, imparting real wisdom, but really you are telling yourself. It was like that. But Vishesh listened too. He is one of the few real listeners I've ever met. Listening is important.

I told Vishesh to watch. I said the way to understand these people was not to listen to me. Listen to them. And watch. Watch until you understand. And then go beyond understanding. Imitate. Become. And then, after that, comes the important part: do it your own way.

I know it's important not to go through life listening to interpreters and commentators, in-betweeners who want to tell you how life works. Experience it for yourself and then, if you want, compare notes with someone you trust. Trust is important, but trust the right people.

I trusted Vishesh.

Vishesh was with me on the dock every day, rain or cold or whatever. He stood beside me and watched. We saw the fishermen going out and coming back. We saw the longshoremen going to their jobs, their ginormous lunch boxes in hand. We saw the tourists getting off their cruise ships, find their shore-footing and hoping to see what they were expecting to see – no surprises please. We talked to them all. It takes all kinds to make a world.

People asked us questions and we asked questions back. That's how you learn. That's one way you learn – questions and answers, follow-up questions, details. You also learn by watching. People talk with their clothes, with their hands, with their eyes. Sometimes I smell fear. A bully usually smells like fear. Or self-doubt. Bullies and cowards are the same that way.

And people asked us questions too. I am not afraid of questions – answering or asking. There are no stupid questions and no new ones either. We invited questions. We were tour guides, after all. We might as well have been wearing cartoon hats with "ASK ME!" signs attached. Or "WAKE UP!" That would have been better.

What's the number one question? "Where's the washroom?" After that one, it gets easier.

One guy came right up to Vishesh and asked him outright to his bare face, "So where's the magic?" I had to laugh, but I saved it for later.

There we were – cannery, fishing trollers, drizzling rain and wet feet and he asks us where's the magic like we would tell him if we knew, like we were magicians who would reveal our tricks. "Oh, it's over there next to the Tim Horton's." I was going to say something, but I caught sight of Vishesh before my mouth could open. Vishesh just bowed his head and touched his chest. I like that. It was like one spirit recognizing another. Talk with your heart. It won't create an argument.

I guess I never said much of any importance to Vishesh. Mostly I just pointed and made up things. "That guy thinks he owns the street, he's got it all figured out, eh?" "That one is always afraid the tsunami's coming, got the escape route all planned." "Beer and hockey. They go together. Problem and solution. Solution and problem."

When that guy asked Vishesh for directions to the Magical Kingdom, I didn't know where to look or what to say. Vishesh's touching his heart was perfect. The tourists love stoic mysticism. It's what they expect. It's part of the package.

For weeks that was our running joke. If we didn't have an answer, we just touched our heart. "When's the sun going to shine?" Touch the heart. "Why does no one want a pedal ride around town?" Touch the heart. "What will we have for supper?" Touch the heart. We touched our hearts and laughed. That's where the answers are. Laughter is a good answer too. As good as any. Better than most.

Together, Vishesh and I were a team. I wouldn't say that we had it all figured out. When does that ever happen? But we had a temporary working solution. We had confidence, but we never knew what we were going to be doing next. That was our motto, the philosophy of our company, the mission statement for our friendship: "Proceed with the confidence that you know nothing."

We knew nothing. And we were able to laugh about it.

I used my partnership with Rusty to learn about this new world. I had seen some of it on the *Marathi Pride*. The card playing, the swearing, the attitudes about women, the drinking and occasional fights were common onboard the ship, but that had been an artificial world, a can of nuts shaken. Everyone was out of their element, thrown together. Most had become so accustomed to life at sea that they knew and wanted nothing else. For me, I was young and took it all in stride.

But now, here in Canada, another level of life was on exhibit for me. Standing on the dock, looking at tourists, I wasn't exactly seeing people in their natural habitat, but still it was a show worth watching.

At Rusty's side on the Rupert wharf, a range of people spilled from those cruise ships – grey-haired couples, honeymooners and adventure seekers. I was seeing their world now for the first time and they had been kind enough to meet me halfway. They were on vacation, strangers here as well, so they easily, unquestioningly took me to be a part of the norm, la tableau de Rupert, as Rusty called it. Like another totem, cedar tree or harbour seal, I was a brushstroke on the landscape, an Indian among Indians – carefully placed and labelled in the diorama of their holiday.

There was in all that one who stood out: a woman, tall, you might also say portly, middle-aged, an American. From her dress and manner, I didn't know what to think. Rusty said she was from California and so quite normal there. What he had to base that on I don't know. She wasn't the first American I had seen up close, but, as Rusty put it, she sure packed a punch, American intense. She walked directly up to us, ignoring the taxi cabs, the shuttle bus and the food vendors. She carried a parasol-style umbrella – I don't know if it was intended for the rain or for the sun. There was neither that day. She jabbed it like a pointer, like sabre, following through with a line of questions.

"How cute!" she cried and then added, "I hope you understand what I mean by cute. No offense intended."

She reminded me of a woman I might have seen in a movie, larger than life, but also playing a part, working from a prepared script, always on stage or before a camera.

"Welcome to Prince Rupert." Rusty offered a tourism brochure and map. "Discover our nature." Rusty repeated the slogan printed on the pamphlet with a gentle wave of his arm, pulling an invisible curtain string to reveal the mountains and forest.

The woman kept her eyes on me, taking the papers from Rusty without looking. "You must be very brave to live here, young man. I mean, don't mind me saying all this, you look very southern, very tropical. I am also inclined that way. How ever do you manage in the snows and colds and whatever else happens here, you poor dear thing." She touched my forearm in protection. "The cold must bite you to the very bone."

She seemed very forward, but likable. "I do my best," I offered.

"Do tell me," she went on, seeming to change the subject, but not, "whatever is there to do here once our ship is gone? You can't spend all your time threading fish hooks or however you get those salmon and other fish."

This was probably the first American I had ever fully met. She might not have been representative of her people, but she was a good ambassador. Within minutes, we seemed to know all about her, although neither Rusty nor I offered up much about ourselves. She had been married at least three times. Pollen, mosquitoes and humidity were not her friends. Money was not something to be chased after – it came to those it chose. She thought poverty was boring. Wealth was irrelevant, but good if you needed to escape. Sea and rail were the only civilized ways to travel in the absence of hot air balloons and zeppelins. And wisdom was not something you should expect to find in a politician, no matter what stripe or colour.

"I have voted both red and blue," she told us. I wasn't at all sure what that meant. I looked at Rusty. He was only smiling, enjoying the theatre. "They're all the same. Give them power and they're gone," she said. "Out the door and on the highway to you know where."

I wasn't sure where this "where" was located. She seemed to be pointing in the direction of Highway 16, the only road out of town. That seemed to fit.

"Now I've got a proposition for you boys." We had been talking – or more correctly, she had been talking – for almost twenty minutes and it had all been a preamble to this one point. "Here's what: if you boys could put together a nice spread of food for me, not that fast food crap." She bit that last word off and spat it out, pointing to the hot dogs and stale sandwiches back along the dock front. "And not the processed designer food like on that ship – good for starters, but a person can get sick of that too. I mean, institutions, when they get their hands on food, they have a talent for turning it into something that just isn't always food, let's face it. And that ship, as good as it is, it's just another institution, a big hotel with a motor and a rudder. And an attitude."

She didn't stop for breath. "You have to know how to talk to those people if you want to get anything beyond the predictable. Anyways – if you boys could find me some real food, something local but real, I would be in debt to you. I could treat you to the same. I mean you find the venue, choose the menu, I'll pick up the tab. How's that?"

DINNER

So it was. We found a place for Mrs. Freeman's dinner. That was her name – Freeman.

People in Canada have such wild, fanciful names. Sometimes their names are meant to tell you their jobs – Brickman and Carpenter, Mason and Stewart – except when you meet them and find out their occupation, it is never anything like that. Anything but. I would like to find a Mr. Carpenter who actually hammers nails into wood. Never – not once. A Carpenter can be an accountant or a taxi driver or a school teacher if he wants. There's no rules. I guess the Western people have broken loose of their castes. Emancipation is a wonderful thing, but confusing.

And then sometimes the names seem to tell you the colour of the person – White, Black, Brown and even Green. Don't trust that either. It doesn't mean a thing.

Anyway, this woman was called Freeman. She clearly wasn't a man with all her parasols and feathers and wispy scarves. And she was not free, even if she called herself a free thinker, a free agent and, once even, a freedom fighter. With all her words, she was as restrained and confined as the temple brahmin or an old johnny up the road complaining to his tea. Still, I liked her and we did our best to make her stay in Rupert a happy one.

We found a bed and breakfast house near the water, a place that was enough a home and enough a restaurant to delight Mrs. Freeman on both counts. Rusty was able to get a big freshly caught coho salmon. He said that was the best kind. They served it up with wild rice and special vegetables. I had never tasted anything like it. And even Mrs. Freeman seemed pleased. We had ourself a feast. It was probably the best meal I had ever eaten that wasn't cooked by my mother.

At the end of the dinner, Mrs. Freeman folded her cloth napkin and put it at her side on the table. She placed her knife and fork on her plate. I did the same. I did it to please her.

"Now, boys," she said, "I have a proposal." It was as if the dinner had been a test and we had passed. The first course was over. Now on to the real thing. "I want to see this land, the heart of it. The real Canada."

"The true north strong and free?" Rusty joked.

"Yes," she said without any humour or irony. "And the real Haida Nation. Not the tourist traps, the photo ops, the emerald glaciers and rainbow sunsets. Show me some magic, the ancient secrets. Got any of those around here?"

Rusty and I looked at each other. I could see Rusty's brain ticking over, going through his catalogue of sights and ceremonies. This was going to take more than a longhouse and few hundred-year-old weather-beaten totem poles.

"We haven't got much time," Rusty ventured. "There's not much really close by. It's a tall order. Doesn't your ship head out tomorrow?"

"I've fixed it. I'll take shore leave," she explained. "They'll go on up to Alaska and see some glaciers. They'll pick me up on the way back down. That'll give us five days." She smiled at us as if to say, "I'm making this simple for you, now do your part." She looked at us each in turn and then spoke again. She made her point as simply and directly as possible.

"Blow my mind," she said.

This might have been the first time I had heard this odd expression. Blow my mind. And then what? I couldn't imagine anyone wanting to have their brain exploded. It seemed drastic, extreme and violent. I sat and looked at her, imagining the mess.

HAIDA GWAII

Rusty was up to the challenge. Where creative income was concerned, he was inventive. There was more to him than just the pedal-rickshaw business. From somewhere, he borrowed a car, got it working. He figured out a budget for gas, ferry passage, motel stay and our fee as guides. Then he doubled it. He told Mrs. Freeman that we would visit the ancients. He told her no cameras allowed, no questions, everything would be explained when we got there.

We didn't lose any time and boarded an overnight ferry from Rupert to Skidegate on Haida Gwaii. The ferry took more than eight hours. It was a long, slow trip. Rusty and I slept on deck. It was all something I was very used to it. Mrs. Freeman stayed in the car.

We drove on to Port Clements on Masset Inset, deep inside the island. It was a long trip it seemed. I don't know if we were lost or if Rusty just wanted to talk to people. At every opportunity, he stopped to ask directions, inquire about road conditions and weather reports. He asked about tides and fishing and people's health. His connections were deeper than I expected. People seemed to know him or a name that he mentioned.

"Is Janice still in Queen Charlotte?" "Is Charles still up to no good, then?" Like that, he felt his way down the road.

After the car had taken us as far as the roads allowed, Rusty had us hiking in the misting rain. Everything was wet, rich with moisture, deeply and fragrantly scented with cedar and moss. There was no sunlight, only the white and grey mists and cloud.

The trees were enormous, towering unlike any trees I had known in India. Those were bushes, bent and bowed by the ocean wind. These Haida Gwaii trees were giants, straight and tall, proud, unmoved by the strength of the sea and wind. They were not plants. They were life forms, species, creatures. We walked at their ankles.

The forest floor was brown with the decay of fallen, rotting wood. This was a rainforest, pure and simple. Ferns were the only green at eye level. You could almost see them growing as you watched. It was like a deep sea floor, another world.

And above us was a canopy, the stretching arms of cedar and spruce and Douglas fir. Rusty did not speak as we walked. We knew to follow in silence, watching our steps, heads bowed. We were in a temple.

I did not know what to expect. But then, there it was. One single spruce tree. A Sitka, Rusty called it, but unlike all the others. In a forest of green and brown, this one tree was golden. Even in the dimness of the fogging mist, this tree glowed. Its golden whiteness seemed to light our faces. It was not like the light of a lamp or a fire, not the tube lights of a shop or a lamp of oil or ghee. It was an inner light, nurturing and holy.

We stood in the presence of that tree. There is no other way of saying it.

I was filled and humbled and then silenced.

Like a protective embrace, I remembered a timeless moment from more than a decade in the past: the beach in Nargol, the woman, the rain, the moment that held me in one spot as this moment was doing now.

Why the two moments should be threaded together I am not sure. The connection was not just the rain. It was the utter peace. On both occasions it had been as if I was looking through a porthole or a viewing glass. As if everything else in life had been distorted and twisted, and now, with the guidance of a sure hand, a dial was turned. Focus was restored.

I do not know how long we stood there, a moment or an hour. I did not want to leave. I wanted to drop to my knees in worship, but I stood. I stood in the stillness.

Then I became aware of Rusty looking at us. He nodded his head to say, "We can go."

I reached out. Bending my knees and, lowering my head, I touched the forest floor with the flat of my hand. It is something Patel would have done.

"Bless us," I said.

RUSTY EXPLAINS

That night at our motel in Port Clement, Rusty explained. "Like a building sixteen stories tall, six meters around, it has a name like a person. K'iid K'iyaas – the Elder Spruce."

I watched Rusty with the fullness of my attention. I was not just listening. I was open to every word. "Kid Keys," I repeated hesitantly.

"K'iid K'iyaas," Rusty corrected. "Say with meaning. Every name has a meaning."

Mrs. Freeman was there also, but was gazing out the window at the gravel parking lot, preoccupied, uncharacteristically quiet.

"It is there. You cannot talk to it, only feel. And it will be there until the end of time."

An eternal tree – I didn't think so, but in that moment it was not a question of thinking, believing or not believing. I had been in the presence of something great. That is all I knew. It was enough.

"His grandfather had said not to look back. But he looked behind to the place they had come."

I wasn't sure what this was related to, what Rusty was talking about.

Rusty twisted at a white package of sugar, turning it over, folding and unfolding, wearing the paper soft with his fingers. He pulled at both ends at once. The package exploded. Sugar went in all directions, but mostly falling in his black coffee and disappearing.

Rusty stirred the coffee with his spoon. "That tree had once been a boy. Now golden, unique, like no other tree in the forest, on the island, or anywhere on this coast, they told him something. 'You will stand here rooted to the earth, birds will fly to you, people will visit you, you will be respected until the final generation, but there will be no communication. Silence, K'iid K'iyaas.'"

Then we were silent also. I don't know if Mrs. Freeman was awed like me or if she was totally bored. I don't know if her mind was blown. Maybe she was thinking of that tree or maybe she was thinking about her California sunshine.

On the car ride back to Skidegate and on the long ferry trip back to Prince Rupert and the mainland, the silence continued. It was only on the Rupert dock, at the sight of her white cruise ship that she erupted into words.

"I would think I should get some of that salmon, smoked and boxed, to take back to Cyril. The boys will love the stories I will have to tell, my adventures away from the ship with real people. What adventures can you have on a package holiday? Another round of bridge, a premium salad bar with twelve choices of dressings, a seat at the captain's table perhaps?"

We waved goodbye to Mrs. Freeman as she rejoined her fellow grey-hairs, honeymooners and adventurers. We could see her reanimated, as she waved from the promenade deck.

Rusty turned to me as we walked away. "You can't do things just so that you will have a story to tell. Life isn't about collecting stories to tell at the card table."

ISLAND

In all this, there was a day near the end of my time in Rupert when Rusty told me something very simple. Like an orca whale surfacing, it seemed to come from nowhere. Then, as you take in the size and the beauty, you realize it is a part of the story, it was there all the time, it had to be said.

We were sitting in a park, really just a bit of grass and a bench, a place to view the harbour. "There is no problem that cannot be overcome," Rusty said. "Problems are all along the path. People think they are land mines waiting to explode under our feet. They're not. They are something normal."

The problems of my life, I really had to admit, had been few. Sometimes I had even felt that my life had been charmed, even watched-over. My greatest enemy had been boredom. Boredom in school landed me in trouble sometimes. Boredom on the *Marathi Pride* had been a mind-dulling tedium, but a solution eventually came. I was saved by creating the lands of my imagination. They weren't fictions. They were my creations. There is a difference.

"My grandfather told me things that I will tell my grandchildren – if I am blessed to have any," Rusty said. "They aren't secrets. The Haida are not a secretive people." Rusty was generous with every-thing.

I listened to my friend with all the fullness that my attention could summon. I hoped, even before he spoke, that I would have something to give back.

"If your roots are strong, if they are intertwined with those of the trees, then there is nothing you cannot overcome. You should not be afraid to believe these things. Look at my people – missionaries and smallpox, church schools, the theft of our land, alcohol. Still we endure. The land and sea endures and we are a part of that. The same. Do not be afraid."

I knew my culture was like that as well. It went back through recorded history. It went back into mythical times, more real and immediate than all the school history books – flying chariots, heroic monkeys, benevolent kings. But now I felt, all at once, in the river of Rusty's words, that his stories and people also went back to a time before time.

I didn't know about smallpox, but I certainly knew about missionaries and church schools. The British Raj, in that moment, became just a scratch on a page in a history book, a footnote to more important things, like a pesky mosquito buzzing around my head. For both of us, Rusty and I, colonial rule had ended before we were born, but we still felt it, an irritation best forgotten.

Rusty pointed to a totem pole in the park. His dancing fingers directed my eyes upwards. Three wooden figures topped the pole, backs together, gazing alert, each in a different direction. "The watchmen," he said, "guardians looking out for the enemy. Sentinels watching all the roads."

"And there is an island out there." Rusty pointed now towards the ocean. "Haida Gwaii, where we went, where the tree stands. We owe our existence to Haida Gwaii. That's our homeland. That is my India. The British used to call it the Queen Charlotte Islands, but they were wrong."

I thought of all the British names in India.

"Who is this Queen Charlotte?" Rusty asked. "Who is this Prince Rupert?"

I felt an anger rising within me. I felt a deep sense of injustice, a wrong done here and in India. And Africa as well. I looked at the guardians atop the pole. Maybe they had missed the approach of the

British, I thought. Maybe the British outwitted and tricked them or maybe the guardians had been sleeping. Or then again, maybe the watchmen knew that it was only another mosquito. Suck a little blood and go away.

Rusty must have sensed the shift in my mood. "You have to forgive them," Rusty said. "Forgive and it is gone."

There was a silence. Rusty was comfortable with silence.

When he spoke after some time he said, "There is another part of Haida Gwaii, to the south from where we were. Do you know it?"

I shook my head, shrugged with uncertainty.

"Gwaii Haanas – Island of Wonders." Rusty looked at me directly. "All these tourists off the ships from Vancouver and beyond, that's what they are looking for. They think they've come up here for glaciers and hot springs, whales and Haida wisdom. What they are really after are the wonders that will give their lives meaning. I wanted Mrs. Freeman to understand something of this by seeing the Golden Spruce, but she couldn't feel it.

"They want an island full of answers, so we offer them Gwaii Haanas. They see the northern lights and they think they are seeing God. They think God is smiling on them when the colours dance across the sky. He probably is. I don't know.

"The truth is that it doesn't happen all the time. The whales don't always swim next to the boat and the lights don't always appear in the sky. But you have to look up or you will never see anything, you will never know if they are there.

"It is this want that keeps us going."

LETTER

When I left Prince Rupert it was not because of Rusty. In fact, I would say that I took a bit of Rusty with me. The same thing happened when I parted with both Patel and Sharma.

It was more because of Mrs. Freeman. She was the cause, the instigator, the reason why I left Rupert and Canada. She was the underwriter. It was a discontent that got me moving. It was Mrs. Freeman who gave me the fuel. I already had the motivation.

It was a day like many others. I was repainting Rusty's rickshaw bike under the cover of a blue tarpaulin. It was raining, but just lightly. The tarp gave a hypnotic glow to everything, a blueness that blocked out the noise of the world. The colour I was seeing was not exactly the colour I was painting. I was content in a temporary kind of way. I knew it wouldn't last.

But still, the care and patience that I gave to the job was unsettled. My underlying feeling, my sense was that the moment would not last. I would probably never use this bike again. I was painting it for Rusty alone.

The pace with which the postman walked did not speak of the importance of the message he was carrying. Mixed in with the bills and advertising flyers, one letter made his entire round of delivery on that day worthwhile. For me, a letter from Long Beach, California, USA was hand-addressed with a green watery ink from Mrs. Freeman's pen. I knew it was from her as soon as I saw the face of Franklin D. Roosevelt on the postage stamp. Mrs. Freeman had the same sort of optimism.

I opened the envelope with a single tear.

"Dear Vishesh," she wrote, coming right to the point, "my time with you was special. I realize this fact only now that I am back home. Here the weather is the same every day, a solid, unchanging sunshine. Every place has its own beauty, I suppose, but Prince Rupert's beauty was special again, in a class of its own, a swirl of spiraling cloud, a mist and a rain that reveals as much as it hides.

"I am painting now, but repeatedly I find my brush reaches for the the greys and blues and greens of Canada, rather than the yellows and reds of California.

"Queen Charlotte haunts me. I do not mean the woman. I do not mean a ghost. I mean your island. I think you called it Haida Gwaii. Is that right? Gwaii must mean island, I realize. We do not have many islands here, only Catalina. And that is so different. Catalina will never haunt.

"Island is such a funny word. Does it mean isolated land? Haida Gwaii seemed so isolated, so remote. I was scared. For me, there was nothing familiar. There was no marina, oceanside bistro or roller bladers with elbow pads. Do you believe it – I was yearning to see surfboards and smell suntan lotion.

"In the face of Awesome, sometimes we are cowards!

"Vishesh, I have also written a letter to Rusty, but I wanted to write to you separately so that I could enclose a small gift for each of you. Please accept it in the spirit with which it is offered."

There was a smaller green envelope within the first. Inside I found a postal money order made out to me in my full name: Vishesh Darshane. I don't know how she knew my last name, but there it was. The money order read: "Three Thousand Five Hundred Dollars U.S."

"My life is coming to an end," Mrs. Freeman's letter continued. "I am going to die, I know that, no matter how many ocean cruises I take. I am not giving up, but I know my money will quite easily outlast my years. God knows, my children do not deserve. They have already taken enough – enough from my bank account and from me.

"I wish you well on your journey,

"Your friend, Vivian"

I looked again at the money order at the foot of the rectangle of stiff paper there was a note written in Mrs. Freeman's fluid hand: "May Wonders Await You!"

Those four words sealed the deal. She understood.

"My life is populated by angels," I thought.

I refolded the letter and, as I placed it back into its envelope, I saw a note on the reverse side.

"Should you question from where my generosity has come (it is not charity), please remember our conversation on the ferry back from Skidegate. You inspired me."

CONVERSATION

I had completely forgotten – maybe because I was so tired, fatigued by our travels and lack of real sleep. We were sitting on the Skidegate to Rupert ferry, both happy and saddened by our return home. Which way was home was hard to tell. That ferry went both ways.

I was looking at the paper cup cradled in my hands, one third filled with cold sweet coffee. I was thinking of my father and his constant teacup friend. To my right, Rusty was already asleep.

Mrs. Freeman sat opposite. She watched the ocean, grey-blue and abstract, and then a white seagull flying along side the ferry, seemingly suspended in one spot as the ferry travelled into the headstrong wind.

"It flies, but gets nowhere," she said. I wasn't sure if she was speaking to me alone, to herself, to the entire ferry. Maybe she was talking to the gull. "Turn around, you stupid bird!" She banged her fist on the thick glass. Her words were addressed to the seagull now, but her tone sounded like she was talking to herself.

"Some birds just tag along. They just take shelter behind some thing or some body. Take a risk, bird. Turn around!" I don't think the bird could hear. There was a window, a transparent wall.

Still, I was in and out of sleep, so not everything was making sense. I put my coffee cup on the window ledge beside me so it wouldn't spill onto my lap. The vibration of the ferry made the surface of the coffee ripple, a small ocean, contained and turbulent.

"I don't know what's worse," she said, "this ferry or that cruise ship."

I thought of the *Marathi Pride*, but I didn't say anything. Had she'd been there, she would have complained even louder – no ship's steward on the *Pride*, no maid service or pastry chef.

"Vishesh." She addressed me directly. I fought to stay awake, breathing in deeply. "Are you going to hang around like that bird, hoping for handouts from tourists – french fries and hot dog buns, hoping for a little mustard?"

"I've seen something of the world," I started. "A bit, some things. In India, I would never have imagined all this. This place is like climbing a ladder up through the clouds. It is like being in a heaven with no Saint Peter saying yes and no. In India there is magic: sadhus and rishis, the deities walk the streets, they are as real as real, as real as you want them to be. When I am here, India is a myth, a storybook land. But when I was in India, this place was impossible, beyond our imagination. Who could have dreamt, seven storey ships alive with lights, whales as long as a bus – and a tree so...." I was stuck, wordless, unable to describe that tree that glowed with an inner light, ancient and wise.

"Get out of here. Take a risk," she ordered. "There are worlds and there are worlds again, each more fantastic. If the gods walk the streets in India, they will walk everywhere. They are not afraid. Monterey or Montreal or Montevideo, go and see. The world's not going to come to you, Vishesh. It's not going to find you here. This is a cut-off backwater."

"No," I agreed. "Yes," I agreed again. And I was asleep.

ROOTS

The roots are in India. For all of us, our roots are in India. There is a deep knowledge of eternity in that land. We are all a part of that, Indian or not. It is a common heritage that reaches back to a time before this time.

I was fortunate to be born there, so I know. It is not just culture or language, a skin tone or a food. Those are all things that are on the surface, like our clothes or hairstyle. It is not the things that we are taught, those things that we display with pride, but which really are meaningless beyond this lifetime.

Roots are those things with which we are born, the values that reach down and deep, they sustain us with a sense of purpose and destiny and meaning. They are our lifeline to the eternal. If we let go of that, we will lose our way. Hang on tight or all the effort will be for nothing.

I am Indian, but I did not know about those roots until I came to Canada. They were always a part of me at every turn and whisper, but only in Canada, when I met Rusty and Mrs. Freeman and so many of the people of Rupert, did I realize that it was something more than curry and cricket, tea and turmeric that made us the same.

Nationality – it is an illusion and a myth devised by geography and politicians and fearful people. It divides more than it unites.

Rusty was a human closer to me than any Indian I ever met. Maybe Columbus was right when he called the people of the Americas as Indians. Rusty and I are the same. We are more than brothers.

Mrs. Freeman knew generosity and kindness better than anyone. She just didn't know how to show it to your face. It wasn't just the money. She was generous from the start. She wanted to share an adventure with us. She freely told of herself without any fear of being judged or ridiculed. She didn't care. It wasn't important.

And that tree, that single towering golden spruce was more spiritual, had more untouched pure divinity than any temple in all of Gujarat.

There are Indians who are very much like me – many of the boys from my school, Sat and Patel and many others. But there are Indians also who I cannot even call my distant cousins. I say it again: nationality is a myth. Spirituality is where it's at – that deep yearning, that tangible hunger for meaning and truth. That is what we shared – Rusty, Sat, Patel and I. That's how we knew each other. We were all seeking the same thing – and it wasn't just happiness.

RUSTY'S LETTER

Years later, when I was back living in Vancouver, I received a letter from Rusty. It was postmarked from Juneau, but the return address said Haidabad. Things had moved on for me and surely for Rusty as well. I felt that even before I opened the envelope.

"Dear Vishesh," it began, "Maybe you heard about the tree." The envelope included a newspaper clipping, almost a full page. "SA-CRED TREE FELLED."

"It was like a murder which hit us all very hard. They say that when a family member dies, it is like a light has gone out. This is how I felt when I heard. You could tell that it was a big thing. People were talking about it even before the newspapers could piece it all together. K'iid K'iyaas was not chopped down. It was weakened, the way a professional faller would do it, cut so that the first strong wind would take take him down.

"That tree was sacred, a part of me – as much as my arm or my leg. It was alive. Its falling was like a drive-by shooting. It just doesn't make sense. The man who did it also disappeared. His kayak was found up the coast. I don't know if he was killed like the tree, but, in my mind, we are all suspects. We all had a motive. People find it so hard to accept things that are bigger than themselves. That tree was big.

"Vishesh, I was back up there a few months ago. There was a white raven around the tree. They said it had been there for several months. People were coming to Haida Gwaii not just to see the tree, but also to see this bird. People called it an albino, but that is not quite right. It was not a freak or an oddity. All ravens were once white until one raven passed through the smoke hole of the long-house and turned black.

"That one bird, they say, seemed to always be around the golden spruce. Perhaps they were talking, talking about the end of days. Then last week the bird was in Port Clements. It was on the electrical transformer near the motel. Remember we stayed there, the Golden Spruce Motel. It stepped in the wrong place or something. All the lights went out in Port Clements. I guess they've fixed the electricity, but that bird is no more.

"Would that have impressed our Mrs. Freeman – a golden spruce and a white raven together. Or would she have just regretted that they couldn't have made her coffee without electricity for the hot water. Some people are always in the dark, electricity or not. They just can't see.

"I hang my head in sorrow for our people because one thing keeps coming back to me. It was said that that one tree would be visited and respected until the last generation of Haida. And now we are no more.

"With you as your friend, Rusty."

The letter was printed from a computer. It had been formatted to fit neatly on a single page, but Rusty had signed his name with a fine-tipped felt marker. He had also hand-written a note in the side column:

"In the presence of greatness, there must always be a suspension of disbelief."

How did I feel? I felt honoured. I felt honoured that Rusty should write to me. I felt honoured that he felt I should know. But, more than that, I felt honoured that I had been among the last people to see the Golden Spruce. I felt honoured to have been in the presence of greatness and to have known where I was standing.

Years later, I heard a bit more, the last chapter of the story. Some people wanted to make a guitar for the country, a Canadian heritage thing. They pieced together a bunch of relics – you know, old rocks, a slice from a theatre seat, Rocket Richard's Stanley Cup ring, a bit of Pierre Trudeau's canoe, a piece of the Bluenose. They even added some wood from a native residential school. Well, the whole sounding board, the whole frontside of the guitar that makes it sound nice came from our tree. The Haida elders wanted the tree to rot away and return to the Earth, but they also blessed this project and donated some wood. And so the tree lives on. The guitar is called Voyager.

Its music must be sweet.

a cart with two wheels

When old words die out on the tongue,
new melodies break forth from the heart;
and where the old tracks are lost,
new country is revealed with its wonders.

Rabindranath Tagore

LEAVING RUPERT

The road from Prince Rupert to Vancouver had always been open for me to travel, an invitation to journey, a route out to the rest of the world. It was as easy as that: head east, turn right at another prince – this one a George – and then down, through the Cariboo and Fraser Canyon to the south coast. Rupert was like that: one way in and one way out. But to actually get up and go was another thing. Maybe I went because I now had the money, a security against the unknown, but there was an even better reason. I went because I had Rusty, an even greater security than money, a friend.

I traded the grey sky of Rupert for the grey sky of Vancouver. The clouds were the same, but what was beneath them was a world apart.

Our vehicle was a big old American car, an enormous station wagon, maximum size, with broad bench seats, broad chrome bumpers, broad everything. This car did not have detail, just strokes and stretches, panels of beige, swaths of brown, handles, cranks and dials.

Changing the radio station took three or four full-wristed twists. Nothing was small, minute or subtle. "The song better be good after all that work you're putting in," Rusty would say. "Getting your exercise, eh, putting that window up and down?"

Another thing that car didn't have was a name – no model name anywhere. No chrome scripted Valiant or tight-lettered Ambassador. We looked. Not finding, Rusty dubbed the car the Mastodon. "It's big," he said, "and it's prehistoric. It must be a mastodon. Extinct or not, she'll get us to Vancouver."

Rusty bought or borrowed or was given the car. He wasn't very specific. Maybe he just found it abandoned somewhere. I don't know. I had the feeling that the Mastodon was something that was always just around, there for the driving, too big for the streets of Rupert, just fine for open road, a boat for the provincial highways.

Extinct or not, to me, this car was the pinnacle of Western luxury, not fast or sporty, more like a house on wheels, steady and solid and very, very long. The first time we turned on the heater a thin veil of steam rose from the dashboard. The steam became a mist, then a fog and then thickened even more. "A swamp stew," Rusty called it. With that, the name Mastodon stuck. "Primordial," Rusty said, rolling down the window, banging the side the car with the flat of his hand. With that and a double whoop, we were off. And I was loving every moment of it.

Rusty drove the full distance down to Vancouver. There is no coastal road, so from Prince George, it's south through the middle of the province – 1500 kilometers, for us more than twenty-four hours on the road with plenty of stops. It was extraordinary, both the scenery and Rusty. He smiled and laughed. His optimism was the smooth pavement under the wheels, the spirit that kept things light. Nothing was a problem, not even a challenge. It was all a joke.

So many things can happen in a lifetime. Why is one thing remembered and not another? What hook or handle gets attached to an event to keep it alive, bobbing at the end of a fishing line always fresh and relevant? Is it random or is the librarian of the brain handing out bookmarks, flagging for future reference. "This moment will be useful in a few years. Remember this one, it's a gem. It will entertain when times are tough."

I wouldn't say that memories change with time. It is a little more than that. They become chalked with fresh experience. The lighting changes. The memory is rotated until a hidden side is revealed.

On that long trip from Rupert to Vancouver, I remember little of the detail. It is as if the lines of the highway, blurred by speed, became one. Where did we sleep? I can guess, but not with certainty. Where were our rest stops, our fueling stations? Unrecorded, lost, except for one. And what were our conversations? Did Rusty teach me slang? Did he talk of politics, current affairs, history or legends and folklore? Did he teach me the whys and wheres of his country, his people, preparing me for the city or did we just listen idly to the radio, singing along where the towns and carefully placed repeater stations allowed a clear reception, singing to each other when the mountains were in the way. Most of it is gone now, filed away in the drawer of irrelevancies, erased to make room for more dramatic or poignant moments.

But with a clarity, raw and clear, I do remember. I cannot forget that hitcher who joined us somewhere around Quesnel or Hundred Mile House. He was an average, nondescript man by most measure, but I can still describe him fully: short but not stocky, a face rough-ened by the sun and wind, but not tanned or cared for, poorly shaved as if a new razor was an unneeded expense and a mirror an inconve-nience. His face was reworked, inexact, like a police suspect sketch detailed by the accounts of too many witnesses. And his eyes – his eyes are the thing that have been given special status in my memory, flagged and footnoted both. His face and body had all the life of a farm fence, but he lived in his eyes. Blue and rich like a windy sky full of busy kites or a pure oasis in an arid desert, his eyes spoke of a different land than his face, hands or clothes.

With this man was an old dog, a companion perhaps, but more likely just there, happening to be travelling down the same road. That dog was like our car: big, old and worn out. His panting was laboured, his breath stale, a steamy fog.

The moment we were on the road with these two, that man started in with his stories. I guess he figured it was part the deal: free passage in return for in-flight entertainment.

Rusty turned off the radio. The dog was asleep. They both knew what was coming. Words.

As the car barrelled south on 97, I sat sideways in the front passenger seat with my arm hooked over the seat. Rusty drove. I watched our passenger. He wasn't a prisoner or a captive, but he was foreign to my eyes, a rare species to be studied. I tried to see the spark of humanity within. I knew it must be there.

To call him a hitch-hiker, isn't exactly right. We didn't find him with a thumb out on the roadside. He didn't hold a folded piece of corrugated cardboard box with the word "VAN" or "SOUTH" scratched and filled in with a felt-tipped marker. We found him at a gas station. His own car cooling and creaking, he asked if we could get him to the the next town and junction. From there, a friend or brother or somebody would help. "Better than paying a small town mechanic," he said.

I continued to fight the feeling that I was looking at a specimen, not actually a person, not a human being like me. He was an odd and strange little man, but who was I to judge. I was a stranger there myself, an alien still by most people's measure, barely in step with the local ways. Still I stared.

He called himself Hop and I have no reason to doubt that that was his real name, except that I couldn't quite get a fix on whether he was saying Hop or Hope or even something like Hopl. He seemed to swallow the end of his words. His accent wandered, unfixed to any one place. He was elusive, shifty.

He told us a lot of stories or maybe just one big long story, stories leading one into the next, connected by a phrase like, "The way that turned out reminds me of the time...." He didn't pause to hear comments or field questions. He didn't ask about us. His stories were populated by charmers after money, monied people after some kind of happiness and unhappy people foolishly pursuing something they thought was love. He was never any of those people, but always the observer passing through, a lone schooner unaffected by wind, current or calls of distress. He was the passive measuring stick. Would we one day end up as characters in one more of his cautionary tales?

"These two hapless drifters seemed to be up to something. I don't know what," he might say. "I feared enough that my own life might be on the line as we sped down that road to nowhere, the foreign one staring at me from over the front seat without relent, while the other, a native guy, kept his bare foot to the floor. They had a scheme, for sure. My only recall against trouble was my dog, pretending to sleep at my side, and the cool blade unseen in my pocket. It wouldn't be the first time I had to fight my way out of trouble."

Yet, for all his talking and story-telling, there seemed to be something he just wasn't getting around to saying, something he was hinting at, but not discussing. Maybe he was waiting for one of us to open that conversational door a little wider.

I made the plunge, but avoided his name. "Mister," I said, "why are you telling? You shorten the road for us, and that's nice, we appreciate it, but what does it all mean? Why are you telling?"

That man looked at me with a penetrating eye. With precision, he drilled through the shell of my being. He reached inside. In that moment, he was like a shaman, a fakir, a man who travels the trails of a dreamtime.

I wanted to break away, to leap from the car or escape the skin of my body. Anything not to be there.

"I am telling you because you are here," he said. "I am here. You are a traveller. I can see that. Your life is that of a wanderer, lonesome, many false starts. You are looking for something. And you don't know what it is, do you?" His stare was unbroken. "You think your confusion is wisdom."

I wanted to break away. To say he was magnetic would miss the point. His stare was a lock without a key, a grip that grasped and tightened without mercy.

"You are destined to travel and search and that is a curse on you. You have lived on land and you have lived on water. You will also live in the air if you need. You have all the elements. They feed into you."

At the edge of my vision I could sense Rusty looking at the man in the rear view mirror. The car was accelerating in an effort to shorten the trip.

"You have seen things that others will never see. You have the vision. You have lived many lives. You are an old soul. You think you can count your lives." He looked out the window, away and away. "You cannot," he said.

He did not move his body, but his face rotated back towards me. He seemed closer now. His eyes narrowed.

"You are protected by wise men who shepherd you in the right direction. I see a man. I see a boy beyond his years, wise. I see a man with authority. I see you in service."

I could feel a chill pass through my body. In the midday heat, in the warmth of the crowded car, I felt a chill. How did he know these things? They were not his to know.

"You are seeking something and you are looking in the farthest corners of the Earth and beyond this world you will also look." He turned his head, cranked down the window and spat, but somehow his eyes did not leave mine. "You're desperate," he said. "You are scared. You're scared it'll take more than this life."

A panic was rising in me. I felt like a thug was ransacking through my personal belongings, overturning my life, invading. I tried to suppress. I tried to calm. Inside I counted.

"You've peeked behind the curtain, boy. Folks don't want you looking there. Just be a good boy now. Behave."

"I don't want to hear," I said. I was firm. I held up the my hand in a gesture of "stop."

"Your palm can tell me more. It's another window."

"Stop!" I said. I might have shouted. Rusty slammed the brakes of the car. It screeched and smoked, dove-tailing slightly.

"Out," Rusty ordered. He reached back for the door handle. "This is as far as you go. There'll be a bus or something. Out."

The man, this Hopl, pulled at his dog's ear. He moved from the car. He did not say thank you or goodbye. "My dog knows your name," he whispered.

Through all this, not for a moment, did his eyes stop drilling.

That man had seen right through me to my inner self. I don't know how far he could have gone. I was shaking. It was like he had been trying to steal something. He had broken in, upset all the drawers, emptied the cupboards, knocked the pictures and lamps, but had not found the valuables. Rusty had arrived just in time and chased him out.

We drove on. "Those kind will blacken your soul if you let them," Rusty said in a calm matter-of-fact way. "Forget him. He won't bother you again. I'm wise to those tricks. I'm your bodyguard, Vishesh. It's not going to happen."

We were silent for a long time.

Somewhere past the town of Hope, Rusty turned the radio back on. I was happy to hear people talk about garbage collection and black bears and hockey players.

VANCOUVER

Rusty had many friends in Vancouver. It was something I wasn't expecting. He had never mentioned any of them while we were in Prince Rupert and I hadn't bothered to ask.

In the north, he seemed to be a lone wolf, but still knowing many people, a good laugh, a joke or a welcoming grin at every turn. In the city, it was much the same. His friends were many. Where did they all come from? On a street or in a store, a buddy or pal could be found. In any random place, Rusty seemed to know somebody. If he didn't know, he introduced and befriended. "Hey, Rusty, how's it goin'? Keeping well?" From the window of a moving bus or across a busy restaurant, it was the same – Rusty was well connected, even popular. It was something I wasn't expecting. A network of people stretched in all directions. Rusty was at the centre.

Although love and friendship was the lifeblood of Rusty's world, a lot of his activities revolved around causes. It was a kind of low level activism and grassroots politics, people power. His basic thinking was that government isn't going to do it for us, so it's up to us – not the individuals, but the people – to make the change, to live in harmony with the land, not to feed off the fat with no concern for the consequence. To enlighten, to educate and to live responsibly is what these people wanted.

Rusty was happy to bring me into his circle of friends and he did it in the most natural and unassuming way. He simply included me in the conversation. Everybody's opinion mattered. There were no dumb ideas. "Come on, Vish," he might say. "An outsider can see the best. Speak up."

I had never been in such a richly mixed community. I came to Vancouver and found the world – a city of immigrants it seemed. Guatemalan refugees, American draft dodgers, Cuban exiles, Soviet refuseniks, Chinese dissidents, Rwandans, Russians and Romanians, each and everyone of them a reformer with an eye on the globe and the ticking clockwork of world events. You could talk about anything and there would be an opinion. Decisions and agreement never came easily. But the choice usually came down to "what should we do, the thing that is easy or the thing that is moral?" It was difficult, but the beauty was that people listened.

They were all there, all the nations of the world, but, apart from Rusty, where were the Canadians? At work? At the hockey game? At home watching American TV perhaps? Then it happened: Frieda.

Rusty introduced us. "Frieda is an artist," Rusty explained. "She works in the gardens with plants and flowers, so she knows about colour. But wait until you see her paint. It's a storm of beauty like nothing else."

FRIEDA

I had planned to stay in Vancouver only a short time, before using Mrs. Freeman's money to move on. I wanted only to take stock before choosing a new direction. Vancouver was to be a stopover, an airport and out. New York, Toronto, London or maybe Dublin – these were my first choices. I wanted somewhere English-speaking – one less obstacle to overcome. But all those plans were overturned by Frieda.

You can lay out a direction, head for a goal with full rigour and enthusiasm and all for nothing. You plan one thing and another thing happens. All you can do is surrender. The forces are unseen. At first you don't know what's hit you. And then you don't care.

I wouldn't say it was love at first sight or the strike of cupid's arrow – nothing of the kind. Frieda and I were placed before each other like opposing pawns on a chess board, the same but different. There was an understanding. You see, it was more than any love. Frieda and I wanted the same thing in life. We didn't want objects or achievements, bank accounts or investments funds. We weren't collectors. We wanted one thing alone: meaning. We were hungry for an answer.

Curiosity can take you a long way in this world. So can generosity and sharing. That's a foundation. Love can be added later.

Frieda had a way with flowers and plants. I envied her creativity. She didn't just consume art and music, culture and life. She lived it and made it.

I suppose in return, Frieda admired my understanding of the stars and navigation. She awed at the numbers, their clockwork beauty, their crisp sparkle.

We would both look at the night sky. "What is that all about?" we would ask. The array of the Milky Way seemed only to be a hint, a glimpse of the wonders beyond – if only our eyes were sharper, our perception unfettered.

I tried to explain cricket, my first love, to her. She listened with intent. But without the game before us on a field, it was difficult to communicate the beauty of its dance. Still, she listened.

Let me say this about Frieda: she wanted to taste it all. She wanted a full serving of life, not just the sliver of a slice dished out by family and school friends, birth and nation and language. In that, we were the same. But I didn't fully know my hunger until I met her.

And here's another thing. This may sound odd. As I came to know Frieda, with each shy and hesitant step, I came to know myself as well. This was all something new for me. I had just never taken the time to meet myself. And it was Frieda who made the introduction.

Frieda was a gardener. I don't mean a hobbyist or a maintainer of flower boxes and windowsill planters. She was a professional, a natural. She was a planter of seeds. A witness, in whose presence life flourished. In the garden of her love, doubt, fear and regret had no chance.

She was a nurturer – a nurturer of seeds, of ideas and of people. She knew when to stand back, when to transplant and, most importantly, when to harvest. Frieda was a gardener, true and strong. She worked in the city parks. In the gardens and wide boulevards and green spaces, she beautified that greenest of cities. She also beautified my life with a touch unmatched. She walked in wonder and brought an ease to the days until they flowed one to the next. She made life both easy and interesting.

Before meeting Frieda, I had been a one-wheeled cart, poorly balanced and wobbling. With Frieda beside me, the cart now had two wheels. When we worked together, the cart moved true and straight. The speed, fast or slow, did not matter because we stayed on the road. I hope that in the smallest of ways I reciprocated and also brought balance to her life. I think I did. We seemed to grow as one.

I can speak at length about Frieda. My wonderment and delight knows no end: her puzzlingly vexed look, furrowed brow and wrinkled nose giving way to a whispering giggle of delight, her uncomplicated way of looking at the world and simple method of sorting the genuine from the false were all endearing. Some might call her a rebel. Her red hair and quick tongue played to that. But Frieda was much more – both more complicated and also refreshingly and directly simple.

There was a moment in all this when I came to know that I had not happened upon an ordinary person. We were looking at kittens in the window of a pet store, a place where we had stopped before, a source of free entertainment. The little cats were pouncing and leaping in mock fierceness, practising their basic hunting skills with laughable awkwardness. Their leaps and miscalculations, arched backs and four-legged leaps were comical.

And then, out of nowhere, disconnected from everything, Frieda turned to me. "Vishesh," she said, getting my attention. She touched my forearm in a way she had, guaranteeing that the attention she had gained was secure and did not wander. "Vishesh," she repeated, "I want to find the truth."

I looked at her, not really understanding. "Me too," I agreed. Agreement was my usual path, the safest way to say the right thing.

"No, Vishesh, you don't understand. The Truth. The one answer. Meaning. I want to find it."

"Okay." I was telling her that I was listening, but little more.

"The truth," she repeated, "Is it in India?"

I tried to remember.

She didn't wait. "I know there are gurus and swamis and all that. But is there wisdom there? Ancient knowledge? It must be somewhere because it's certainly not here."

I looked back at the cats. I wasn't used to this kind of conversation. I felt a little out of my depth, but I didn't want to show it. "There's the *Bhagavad Gita*," I offered.

"I don't mean in a book. I've read enough books. The Whole Earth Catalogue is about the only one worth keeping and that's for the recipes. I don't want a recipe or a prescription. I want an experience. Real truth. Genuine. The kind that lasts, not just for a few days like a drug or a new toy. I want the kind of truth that changes everything."

"Do you mean bliss and joy?" I was trying to be funny, but she didn't get it.

"Yes, bliss and joy, Vishesh. Take me to the joy."

I pointed, with mock simplicity, at the kittens pawing the air and skittering across their enclosure. She looked and smiled. She gripped my hand and smiled again. Wrinkling her nose, she laughed.

Frieda, I decided at that moment, was special. By the end of the month we were married. I wasn't going to let her go.

APARTMENT

Life just kept happening. New things, new people emerged from nowhere and, now as an adult, I was still trying to find the best way to dodge these new style cricket balls and ear-tweaks. We often live our lives in the not-long-ago-past, not quite catching up to now. Or else we are racing ahead, arranging the furniture for that ideal life in tomorrowland.

Frieda ended all that for me. In so many ways, she brought me soundly into the present. She demanded an immediacy and nowness to everything. She was spontaneous, never wanting to do anything the same way twice. "Remember that for next time" was not in her vocabulary. For her, there would never be a next time quite like this time.

Frieda and I took an apartment in Vancouver – a damp and moldy basement flat, a bachelor suite they called it. Either way, it was a subterranean hideaway, our refuge from the world. The rent was low. The landlord was either ignorant of the exorbitant prices being charged in the neighbourhood and throughout the city or maybe he just took pity on us. He might have thought us to be refugees or exiles. He said little and we kept our side of the deal with the same silence. The rent was frozen at some depression era level and we wanted to keep it that way.

We didn't make trouble. We did not complain about the dripping faucets, the mice or cold drafts. We made do with what we had and did our own repairs as best we could. Our first investment was one of those pet store kittens, a frontline warrior in the great rodent wars.

Frieda's modest part-time income paid our rent and fed us. Her skillful navigation of the secondhand stores kept us clothed in a fetching but slightly out-of-date kind of way. We fancied ourself ahead of the fashion cycle, not slightly behind. Frieda knew her city and was happy to show it to me. She was my teacher in the ways of this new world.

WALK

Vancouver is a beautiful city. Or let me put that another way: it is a very ordinary city in a beautiful setting, a jewel greatly enhanced by its placement, an average painting well-framed. There are about thirty or forty other cities on this continent of the same size or larger. Many are on the ocean. A few are nestled on the sides of mountains. Only Vancouver has both of these virtues at the same time. On the first fjord of a labyrinth of a coast that stretches north to Prince Rupert and beyond into Alaska, Vancouver sits in a catbird seat – front row for the American show to the south, but out of the way should trouble start. This is what Frieda told me.

And yet, in the earliest of mornings, as I sat on the beach, I could only feel a deepening calmness. With the city still asleep behind me, how could I say that this inlet, this stretch of sand was any different than any other inlet, cove, driftwood-covered shore anywhere on that long coast? In the hand of nature, Burrard Inlet was no different than Rupert's Hecate Strait. Did God favour one over the other? In that moment, I was in Nargol. It was Dar es Salam in reverse, the sun here setting into ocean rather than rising from it. Nature is calming. She also forgives.

"You can't live only on the idea of mountains and ocean," I once said to Frieda, challenging her idealism.

"I can if I want" was her quick reply. I believed her again. The point she was making is that nature nurtures. It feeds and strengthens. It doesn't sap and drain.

"Plant a flower, let it grow," Frieda was fond of saying. "It will tell you about life. It will make you feel alive. A plant will teach you how to reach out, how to grow, how to survive."

Vancouver was like that for me: a city calmly carrying on. It was ordinary and at the same time special. I liked that. I watched and learned.

If I was confused, Frieda would explain. Or better, she told me to suspend my disbelief. "Grant a blanket amnesty to all your doubts," she suggested. "Tell all your concerns to go away. Pardon and forgive. Look for the good and it will show itself."

So that's what I did. Some things were odd. Some things were weird. Some things were not what I was used to and some things just seemed wrong. I forgave all that and told it to go away. I turned my attention to the good and there I found Frieda waiting for me.

"What is this place?" I asked Frieda one day as we walked the seawall in Stanley Park. "What is this Vancouver, this Canada? The people don't agree, but also they don't argue either." I had been used to Indian Hindus and Muslims at each other's throats with violence or threats of violence, warring factions assaulting or stubbornly ignoring each other, people and non-people. If the British had treated Canada as they had India, there would have been an ugly partition: two countries, Canada and Quebec. As it was, these two peoples lived in one place. If Quebec left, I doubt if there would be a war, just bad feelings. "These Canadians," I thought, "are either very odd or very great."

"They are all just like us." Frieda waved her hand before us like she was holding a magic wand or was cleaning a blackboard. The cyclists, skateboarders, joggers and walkers came to the service of her words. "They are all the same, looking, figuring, chasing. Some want perfect health, so they jog. Some want a perfect job, so they work, chasing some promotion. Some want money, so they squirrel it away. But they all want love. Simple love. They want to be told they're alive. They want the approval of their neighbour. They want to be told they mean something. And they want to create meaning. It's all the same. They want love."

I agreed. It seemed obvious, even simple.

"Vishesh," Frieda continued, "There is no Canada. Vancouver is just another place in the world. And this place, we've named it after and in honour of a English sailor with a Dutch name. How relevant is that? He's long gone. Never lived here. Left his name and shoved off."

I thought of Nargol and Bombay. I wasn't sure what those names meant. Then I thought of Prince Rupert and smiled. If Boye was barking and catching bullets in this park, he'd would have to be on a leash.

Frieda was still talking. "God or somebody or some thing made this world – or maybe it just happened, I don't know. Humans added the names and numbers. We drew the lines to separate us from them, ours from theirs. And we didn't do a very good job of it."

"Vancouver." Frieda waved again. "What kind of meaning does that give us? Let's all be sailors, make a map, stick our friends names all over it and go home and die. Do you know what Canada means? Some European asks, 'What do you call this land?' The native guy, from the Iroquois, says, 'Canada.' It turns out that that means 'my village.' It has no meaning. It's like asking, 'Where are you from?' 'Ah – my town, eh.' But that's what I like. Canada is everybody's town. Welcome home, Vishesh. Home, sweet home for everyone.

"The Spanish and Portuguese came looking and couldn't find any gold or silver so they wrote 'acá nada' on their maps. That means 'nothing here' – a canada."

"So if we are in a country whose name has no meaning," I offered, "we have to create our own meaning."

"Exactly," Frieda laughed, rubbing her hand together. "We have to look deeper. Inside ourselves we'll find meaning. There is a town on the prairies called Qu'Appelle. Do you know what that means?"

I shrugged. "It sounds like one of those woolly hats."

"It means 'who calls.' Isn't that great? The whole country should be called Qu'Appelle. A question for the ages – we'll draw the lines, make a country, you figure out what it all means. Figure out who is calling and

you've got the meaning of life. The problem is that most people are so wrapped up in getting their cool kitchens and fast cars that they don't hear anyone calling. They can't hear the calls for help, the calls for peace. They can't even hear their own spirit calling. That's how noisy their lives are."

I loved Frieda when she was like this – on a roll, teasing out every aspect of the world, questioning everything. Zero in and – bullseye.

"Nations are a crock of lies," she shouted. "Give the people a flag, a piece of cloth with some nice colours, give them a team to root for and they think they are unified. It's a crock."

"It is a maya," I said slowly, "an illusion, something to believe in."

"Precisely," Frieda said. "I have more in common with you and you are from the other side of the world. Go figure. We are strangers here, Vishesh. Both of us. It's just that I have a citizenship card.

"Maybe countries should be something different." Frieda was becoming serious. "All the greedy people could go to one place and have a flag full of dollar signs. All the angry people could go to another place and shout at each other. All the big egos could go live on mountains and each sit on a different peak.

"I'm tired of it all," she said. I thought it was laughter at first, but she was almost crying. We stopped and sat on bench. For a long time we were silent.

She was looking out at the ocean, the inlet and outer harbour. "When are they going to realize there is only one world, not a two hundred or two thousand? We need to call a truce so we can start looking for the truth. These illusions stop us from seeing. They shelter and protect, but they also obscure. When are we going to be strong enough to take it full on?"

I tried to comfort her. Her tears were real.

FRIEDA SPEAKS

Vishesh is like no one else. He is sweet and kind. He listens with his full attention. He is cautious and he is brave, both at once. His values are deep. They are not of the moment or motivated by his needs or wants. He is not selfish.

Vishesh does not know himself. He is the group, the family, the community, the world before he is Vishesh. When Vishesh travels, he does not change. He is the same person no matter where he stands.

But Vishesh also learns and grows. He is a part of every person he meets. With equal measure to all, his love is served. It is not parceled out in return for favours or love in return.

Vishesh has told me of his mother and father, his brothers and sisters, of a man named Patel, a boy called Sat, a ship's captain who was kind and a kind patron in California. Rusty I have met. He is my friend as well. I call him "brother." I have never been able to use that word with such ease.

So many have touched Vishesh's life and he welcomes each with the same love. To him, love is a river that flows in two directions at the same time.

Of all the people in all the stories of his life, Vishesh holds the highest love for his mother. When he speaks of her, I can tell that she has filled his heart with wonder. I can see her, although we have never met. She has told him tales and stories that have each imparted a lesson or a value. They are signposts to help him through life. And each is wrapped in an adventure so that it is remembered at the right moment.

I sigh deeply for what I do not have. Vishesh comes from a world rich in stories. And the stories are truths. When he speaks, I can tell. Beneath the surface of his words are kings on battlefields, virtues defended, honour maintained. The difference between Vishesh and me is simple. I know right from wrong because I have thought it out. I have weighed the pros and cons, made a list, weighed the choices and made a decision. Vishesh simply knows. My values shift depending upon who I meet, where I go. Vishesh only continues to know. He is strengthened by travel, but he does not change inside. I want to know like that also.

Vishesh wears an invisible cloak called dharma. The wisdom of ages tells him right from wrong. It is a code of conduct not unlike a knight. Vishesh is chivalrous, but not because of knighthood. It is his path. Dharma gives him balance.

Vishesh makes mistakes. But, more importantly, he makes corrections.

In my view, Vishesh is impeccable. He is like no other. And I am now his wife.

I asked him to marry me. I only said the words because I felt he wanted to say them, but was unable. It was not shyness or a failing of character on his part. I just wanted to help. So I spoke first.

He said yes. Without hesitation, he said yes. But he said first he would seek the permission of his parents. This made me love him even more. Vishesh does what is right.

Vishesh said we will go to India when we have enough money. He said we will marry again when we get there. That marriage will be for his family, his school friends, everyone who can attend. Their presence and their blessings will be our protection.

I am nervous and unsure. How can I measure up to the expectations of his family? Vishesh says there is nothing to fear because his mother will accept me. She will love me because he loves me. Everyone else will follow his mother.

Vishesh is for me. I have never met anyone like him.

There are many I could marry and still be happy. I could travel the length of my life with this man or that man or no man at all and arrive at the same destination: happiness.

But I want more than happiness.

HOME

Our apartment was hidden. As if in a secret cave, we were not easy to find. Frieda called it a parallel universe. I thought of it as a sanctuary.

The house itself was huge. Once a rambling mini-mansion built on a corner lot in an old neighbourhood, it dominated the street with its bay windows and decorative dome, a weathervane on top reaching for the wind. Over the years, this once single family home had been divided and subdivided into a collection of flats. Small apartments for single students and young couples were cut into what had once been single bedrooms, sitting rooms, even a dining hall still intact with a chandelier hanging over a single futon mattress spread centre on the hardwood floor. Milk crate bookshelves and thumb-tacked posters replaced side tables and oil paintings.

In the vestibule front entrance of the old house, there was an array of buttons, an old intercom system connecting to each of these small homes-within-a-home. There might have been twenty black buttons in total, some inoperably stuck, broken or disconnected. Others were intermittent or temperamental. The voices always sounded the same no matter who was talking. Next to each button was a neatly typed label. 7-E Tanner. 6-B basement. 4-F Scarfe. A-3 Occupant. I suppose the numbering system once made sense, but now, with renovations and time, it was a cypher encrypted to confuse. E5 do not disturb.

When you pushed our button – W-3X Darshane – it made a clear and quick connecting buzz to the wall panel in our suite. From there, we could release the lock, admitting any visitor into the house. But that was little help. Directions were also needed. You could wander the halls and stairs as much as wanted, you would never find W-3X. And I doubt if any of the tenants, if you asked them, if you happened to run into them in those stale hallways and drafty stairs, could tell you where we were with any certainty. "Are you sure you have the number right?" they might ask. Or maybe they would guess, "Try the attic rooms, back that way."

To get to our apartment, you needed to leave the house altogether. You needed to go back to the street and then to the rear garden by way of a narrow path fitted between our house and the next, roofs almost touching, an unintentional cover from the rain. In the overgrown, poorly-kept communal backyard was a small garage built into the basement of the house, now disconnected from the road by a fence, something of a lawn and a line of cinder blocks.

Inside the garage, sometimes lit by a single, bare light bulb and even when empty too small for any modern car, were boxes, construction supplies, paint cans and the unwanted debris of life, too big to discard and too worthless to sell. Otherwise there was nothing: no door, no window, no curtain. But there were hinges, the hint of an entrance, and a loop of rope that served as a door handle. If we knew you were coming, that section of wall would swing open with a warm welcome.

I remember the first time Rusty came by. "Hiding out from Mounties, Vishesh? Or are you just shy?" Rusty laughed. "Witness protection maybe."

NOTEBOOK

It was in that basement apartment, our first home, that we started both our marriage and the notebook. It was a day that seemed like most others, neither a holiday or a feast day, grey like the skies, without merit or disappointment. But, by the time it was over and the last house light turned off, the last candle extinguished, the day felt historic. In many ways it was the cornerstone of our marriage, a turning point from which everything else radiated, a foundation. It was our day of liberation. Independence Day, Frieda called it.

The idea, as Frieda explained, was that the notebook would be one part journal, one part scrapbook, but many parts a registry of wisdom. It would be a clearinghouse, you could say, a way to understand the course of our quest. She called it that – a quest. With all the imagery of knights and grails and battling dragons, she set us out on a noble and virtuous venture, a quest, not for a grail in an age of chivalry, but for truth and meaning in an Age of Wonder. For Frieda, life was for adventure.

"And, you know," she explained to me, "in one story, the knights found their Holy Grail in the most unlikely spot. After roaming the hills and living rough and risking their lives in foreign lands, the grail was just there – " She pointed across the room and I looked "— under the Roundtable. It was there the whole time. So we have to look everywhere, Vishesh. Everywhere. No excuses."

I ducked my head under the kitchen table. "Roger, Sherlock. Nothing here."

That modest little blue-lined book became our road map. It was our chronicle, a hope chest, our confessional and our guide. This little volume – really only a school tablet scribbler – was our atlas to finding the truth. Our premise was the belief that meaning was somewhere and it was ours to discover. To find it, clues needed to be recorded, details listed. We were young and underemployed so we had a lot of time – time for seeking and time for fun as well.

We decided that we couldn't just go up to people and ask, "Have you seen the truth around here?" or "What is the meaning of life?" We had to be more discerning. Frieda said we needed some test questions, some way of screening. "There are people in this world," she explained, "some are evolving and some are devolving. The ones who are going down want to take you with them. We want to avoid that crew at all costs. The ones who are going up are the ones we want to find. They're our people, Vishesh. They're the seekers."

"It all has to do with desire." I remembered Patel once saying something similar.

"That's right. If we desire the truth, we'll find. One way or the other."

I was okay with the one way. I was unsure what Frieda meant by the other way.

"Of course," Frieda said, "the biggest group aren't going anywhere, up or down. They're happy with what they have – double-door fridges, four-wheel drives and six-packs in the cooler. They're nice company, good for a dinner party, but they're not going to know what we're talking about when we ask about truth. For them, truth is the right answer on a business college entrance exam. Everything they want is for this life only.

"Vishesh, we need to have some questions so that we know who we're talking to. We don't need people with their eyes on tomorrow. We need people with an eye to the eternal."

I agreed. It didn't take much to agree with Frieda when she spoke like this. "How about: 'What is the spirit? a) a ghost, b) your eternal Self, or c) a drink of whisky.'"

"That's good." Frieda began to transcribe my words. "Multiple choice makes it easy to mark."

I don't know where Frieda found the notebook, but as it filled with our writings, she found more, cheap but elegant scribblers, identical in every way, but each in a different soft colour, hues of blue and forest green. At first, she clipped them together and then grouped them into cardboard slipcovers of her own making. The notebooks were numbered and then indexed, each slipcover decorated in a collage, bits of magazines, newspapers, fabric and texture, whatever would stick and please.

The notebook – it was always "the notebook," singular – was more than a diary or journal. A diary is the private work of a historian. It records the day, but without revision or interpretation. Our notebook looked forward. It prepared our path into the future. It was a scout calling, "Coast is clear, this way now." In it we wrote inspirations, meditations, jokes, promises to ourselves, the wisdom of great writers, philosophers and sages. We recorded snippets of overheard conversation, transcribed graffiti, song lyrics and poetry. The notebook was our life. It was the outer edges of truth, hints of the eternal, rays of pure sunlight filtered through the confusion of the days. It was the thing that kept us on course.

On that first day, Frieda placed that first notebook on the table. She opened the cover and flattened the centre with her thumb. Like a Japanese tea ceremony or an investiture into a secret society, she chose our best pen, an ultra-fine tip, micro-point, waterproof ink marker and wrote an inscription. She recapped the pen. With ritual exactness, she rotated the notebook clockwise with both hands, fingers stretched and straight. I read her words.

"Let it be known that we know nothing."

I smiled at her in agreement. "Perfect."

"Write something." She handed me the pen. "Make it real. It has to carry us to the end."

I hesitated, adjusting the pen in my hand to find the best grip. I was on the spot, but I could rise to the occasion.

I wrote: "May we proceed with that confidence." I added: "Surrender does not mean giving up."

It was like a new ship had been launched. Slipping gently into the sea, its maiden voyage, its only voyage, began.

Frieda unwrapped a small chocolate bar, gave it to me with two hands and a bow of the head. I took it and broke it in half, returned a portion to her with equal grace and ceremony. Hard at first, then soft and sweet and cool, we both enjoyed. Our pact was sealed. Our journey began.

Our plan was simple. Whatever we might do in life was fine as long as it pleased us and did not bring us regret or sadness. Work, school, play, entertainment or even idleness – the activity didn't matter. What was important was the notebook and the seeking. We had a goal. We would return to the book to measure our progress. We would get there together, with each other's help.

For some, marriage is a compromise. It is the end of dreaming, the death of ambition. For us, it was a new beginning, a new day, a chance to start over, alone no more. The past was forgiven. We proceeded with confidence. We knew nothing. And more important: we knew that we knew nothing.

For me, getting married was like walking through a door and out into the world. I had heard about the outdoors, maybe seen it through the window or from the reports of others, but now I was there, actually outside, with the people and with Frieda. That's what it felt like. Everything was the same, but I saw it differently. Not only was I seeing through my vision and understanding, I also now had Frieda to explain. She had a different take on almost everything. Together we could do it.

I was feeling this newness of direction during those first days. I was in the apartment alone, awaiting Frieda's return. The notebook was on the table. I reread our dedicating inscriptions. I turned the page and saw that Frieda had written a third.

"A traveller's guide to the new world: Life on Five Questions a Day.

"Take nothing for granted. See the beauty in everything.

"Do we want to be a drop or do we want to be the ocean?"

DISCOVERY

Vancouver is a city of bridges and water, a peninsula with a river to the south, a deep inlet to the north, a natural harbour, the reason for the city being. The tip of this peninsula is a place of beauty, a natural refuge from the city, a park called Pacific Spirit, the site of an enormous university and a favourite spot to which Frieda would often take me. It was a convenient wilderness, a short bus ride from our home, a getaway of little effort.

Walking in the woods, within sight of the university, but still with the ocean breeze and salt air around us, we talked, as always.

We had been to the beach that day. I remember because I was carrying a twist of driftwood on my shoulder, occasionally dragging it along the ground. Frieda might have been speaking about totem poles or poets' souls or beach barnacles or any number of things. It was all the same, a search for meaning or for a pattern, connections and causes. I was listening.

Frieda was fond of talking, but she would often also ask me to explain. I suppose she thought that I was teaching her about the ways of the East, the wisdom of the *Gita*, dharma, karma and the brahmin temperament, Something like that. I was the patient man who knows the eternal wheel of life. But in any one of her questions, there was more wisdom than all my answers put together.

"Why is God so patient with us when we make the same mistakes over and over?" Or: "What is freedom? The freedom to be stupid? To do nothing? If we have free will, why don't we take the opportunity to rise above it all?"

One of the things about being an immigrant is that you can pick and choose. Hang on to the ways of the old world if they are good or let them fly away and go with the new. The wise immigrant can straddle both worlds to good advantage. This I was learning: pick and choose.

Frieda stopped and looked at me fully. She always had a way of bringing a question home. Never satisfied in blaming others for the state of the world, she questioned herself first. "Vishesh, are you even listening? I said I am not doing my best."

She might have thought I was ignoring, looking past, avoiding. "Vishesh," she repeated with a sharp even stern stage whisper.

She was right. My attention was gone. I was looking past her, down the path into the woods. There was something there that was not a tree. It was a statue, a bronze bust, head and shoulders, bearded, Rabindranath Tagore waiting for us.

"I do not put my faith in institutions," the plaque read, "but in individuals all over the world who think clearly, feel nobly and act rightly. They are the channels of moral truth." A single garland of threaded marigolds was respectfully draped around his neck, slowly dried by the gentle forest sun. Tagore was calling. "It's Saint Rabi of the Rainforest," I whispered.

"It's a sign," she said. "A sign," she called to the trees. "Thank you." We were both delighted in the whimsy of this omen well-placed.

"Here we are on the path and a wise man is pointing the way," I said.

"Exactly. And which way is he pointing?" Frieda asked. The path forked at the statue. "And more than a wise man, I'd say. More like a decorated saint."

"It doesn't matter which way we go," I said, reading the plaque again. "He says we are channels of moral truth." We danced around the statue, laughing.

"Rabindranath, the patron saint of our journey," Frieda sang.

TAGORE

It was probably only a few days later that Frieda took me on another hike. It was a public trail, signposted and marked with triangular fluorescent markers. The spot was a favourite of hers, but it was some time since she had last been there. "It will take some effort, but it'll be worth it," she promised.

We were soon climbing steeply through the trees. What at first had been an urban trail with young children, dogs and mountain bikes, soon became sparsely travelled, almost empty. The steps and short bridges became less maintained, rotting, then non-existent. The trail markers were no more.

As our ascent steepened again, our conversation shortened to intervals and then stopped altogether. We were tired. It was afternoon before we reached a clearing, the first real view we had seen all day. On the bald rock face we rested and ate. Below us, the carpet of treetops spread thick to the water, an inlet of the ocean, reaching deep inland, far from the open sea. The city was out of sight, distant but still present around the corner, a distant hum.

With my shoes loosened, I was almost dozing. Frieda started to speak.

"Do you think being in the right place at the right time is important?"

"I guess. Yes."

"Is it a matter of the gears all clicking into place before anything is revealed or do you think that fate finds you, no matter what?"

There was a long silence.

Frieda again: "Do you think this is the right time, the right place?"

"Patience is important," I said. "Everything with time."

"What if that Tagore of the statue really wanted to speak to us, could he reach out? Would he have to write us a letter long before we were born, before he died, post it to us, wait until it was delivered?"

Frieda's universe was filled with what-ifs. She always wanted to change the rules. She didn't want to play the game that everyone else bought into. "Frieda," I said. "When you play cricket there can only be eleven players on a team. There can only ever be eleven players. That does not change. There can be only one batsman at a time. If I hit the ball, it has to land on the ground. I can't knock it into next week's game. If you want to play the game, you have to accept the rules."

"Why?"

The way Frieda said "why" was never a roadblock. It was never the end. It was always the beginning. Her whys were her way of hitting the ball beyond the boundaries that no one else could see. Her one "why" created ten "what-ifs."

"What if we could talk to Tagore? I mean really talk to him. What if we could say, 'What did you mean, what were you talking about, what did you know?' Would he answer? And not just in our imagination. Really. What if we could talk to William Blake and Wordsworth and Lao-Tzu and Buddha and all the long forgotten saints and poets, wouldn't they want to talk to us, talk to us so that we could remember all the things we have forgotten?"

"Do you want to have a seance, Frieda?" I sat up. "Do you want a visitation, a burning bush? This is a good spot, on top of a mountain and everything."

"Don't make fun of me. This is serious."

Frieda glared at me. "I'm talking about trust," she said. "Trust yourself. Desire the truth. This isn't about magic or dreams or drugs. None of it. This is about knowing, asking and receiving. You've got to be pure in your desire, still. No ripples. No thoughts. Listen with your heart."

I was quiet and without thought. It was perfect. For a moment. Frieda spoke again.

"I have been reading Tagore," she said. "He wrote a book called *Gitanjali*. It means Song Offerings."

"I know Tagore," I said. "They taught him in school. He wrote the national anthem."

"Do you know *Gitanjali*?"

"Some," I said.

"I've been reading." Frieda pulled our notebook from her bag. She leafed through the pages. "He wrote the poems in Bengali. They are amazing. Devotional in every way. Deep and humble."

I nodded in agreement.

"But that's just the beginning. I've been finding out about him. He was about fifty, travelled to England with his adult son. This was in 1912. An unknown poet, unknown outside of India, on this long sea journey. Can you imagine the distance, the time, the boredom?"

I could. Very well. I closed my eyes and lay back on the rock, cool to my back, the warm sunshine above. The sunlight danced colours on my closed eyelids. I listened to Frieda's story, the beauty of her voice.

"To pass the time, he continued to translate his own poetry, from Bengali to English, line by line. Maybe it was like doing a jigsaw or a crossword, something to pass the time. He had been ill before departing on this big trip, India to England. It was a part of his recovery. He needed both to pass the time and to be in full creative spirit when he arrived.

"A timepass," I offered.

"Or maybe he was brushing up on his English, preparing for his arrival in London. He had been there before, but many years had passed."

I could hear a ship horn far below us on the inlet, out of sight, but clear in tone. I remembered the long days on the *Marathi Pride*, boredom which made time stop, the clock the same every time you looked at it. Bengali to English, word to word, some fifty pages, one hundred and three verses and then he reworked them again to regain the poetry and song, not literal, not rhyming, but still poetic and heartfelt.

"Where words come out from the depth of truth

Where tireless striving stretches its arms towards perfection

Into that heaven of freedom, my Father, let my country awake."

He was translating himself for himself only, he said, an exercise as he set out across the Arabian Sea. I wish I'd had his words to comfort me as I had travelled those same waters.

"Like a flock of homesick cranes flying night and day back to their mountain nests let all my life take its voyage to its eternal home in one salutation to Thee."

I could hear the birds. I could hear the devotion.

GITANJALI

Tagore arrived in London with his son and daughter-in-law. The small notebook of poetry, his first efforts in the art of translation was tucked into his briefcase. And then the shock: his son, Rathindra-nath, left it on an underground train. Forgotten, abandoned and lost in this foreign land.

The son was devastated. His neglect, his lack of attention was a failure to his father. He didn't know what to do, who to turn to. What else was in the case – travelling papers, addresses, a book or two, a bit of money. All seemed replaceable compared to the note-book of poetry, endless hours of careful composition.

Rabindranath and his son are telling the story to an acquaintance, a painter, William Rothenstein, a kind man and a creator of fine portraits. He was their host in England. Rabindranath had met him years before in India. William's love of India and her ancient culture had brought the men together. His invitation brought Tagore to London.

"And then there was a knock at the hotel room door," the son explained, transported by his memory of the moment. "This English gentleman simply, a true gentleman, handed us the case. He had found it on the tube and somehow found us. Returned it without thought of reward or compensation. This England is not a bad place. There are good men here as well. Like India: both good and bad together."

Rothenstein became interested. "And what in this case was causing you so much concern?"

The son looked to his father. Rabindranath did not speak. "*Gitanjali*," he said, turning back to Rothenstein. "My father has been translating."

"Really?" Rothenstein interest was heightened. "You took my suggestion then. Literal translation is insufficient, but from the hand of the poet and, in this case, the author himself – ah, well, then we have something." He knew that Tagore was a poet of some talent and stature in India, but he had never been able to see for himself, not being able to read Bengali. "May I...?" he asked.

"It is nothing. It was only a timepass for the voyage. Time moves slowly on a ship. I thought revisiting those lines would be a way to prime the pump, to coax some fresh verse to the surface. I had been ill before the voyage. It was an effort to regain my health. Unless the brain is fully active, one does not feel strong enough to relax completely. The only way to keep calm was to take up some light work. I took the poems of *Gitanjali* and set to translate them one by one. I simply felt an urge to recapture the feelings that had created such a creative satisfaction within me. The pages of the small exercise book came to be filled gradually."

"Sir, it would be a great honour for me. I have only known your writing by reputation, never through first hand experience. Grant me that gift that only your countrymen have been privileged to read. I can return it to you before the week is done, I guarantee. Perhaps I can repay the favour in some small way – a tour of the academy, the India Society, some introductions, whatever you wish during your stay."

With reluctance, mostly born from Tagore's humility, William Rothenstein left with the notebook in his pocket. "They are nothing, only an exercise to break the tedium" were Tagore's parting words.

That night and again in the morning, Rothenstein read and reread the poems. "As poems, they are grand. As hymns of praise and devotion, they are fantastic, without equal in our country. We have lost touch. The writings of saints no longer interest us. It has all become stale. But these words should be sung from the steeples, preached from the pulpits. These poems are inspired."

He had the notebook copied. Three typed manuscripts were passed on to three men of influence and prestige. The first two were enthusiastic. The third was ecstatic. That man was William Butler Yeats, the poet.

Hastily, Rothenstein arranged a reading in his home. The guests would come to hear Yeats, but the words would be those of Tagore.

TAGORE SPEAKS

I do not remember ever hearing English for such a long time without interruption. And on top of that, it was my own words.

Mr. Yeats reads well. He is used to public speaking. He commands the stage and has the respect of his audience. But still, it might have been better if they had interrupted, spoken out, stopped it all, or at least smiled or frowned. It was like a wall, the blank faces. Boos and calls would have been better than that silence. But once started, there was no other course.

The evening was entirely Mr. Rothenstein's doing, but Yeats was instrumental. He drew the audience and carried the weight. For me, I was, I expect, ignored, an embarrassment, an exotic, a bit of an inconvenience.

Yeats did not read all of my *Gitanjali*, only selected poems of his choosing, but each translated by myself. As I listening, I also edited and retranslated in my head. "Not that word, another, but there is no English, Bengali knows the nuance, English is so broad."

I don't think they knew what to make of me. Even in India, my height sometimes brings some people to a standstill. I am odd in their eyes. In London, my kurta and shawl, my dark skin are added. My beard hides me. My accent bites at their language.

My son was there, dear Rathi. He sat at the back of the room, chair against the wall. He looked uncomfortable. I directed my attention to him. It made it easier. His was a face I understood.

"Time is endless in thy hands, my lord." Mr. Yeats reading is both commanding and humble. He understands.

"There is none to count thy minutes.

Days and nights pass and ages bloom and fade like flowers.

Thou knowest how to wait."

But do they understand, these men of English, published critiques, critics and essayists themselves? Do they know God?

"At the end of the day I hasten in fear lest thy gate be shut, but if I find that yet there is time."

Was there applause? It was slow in coming. It was polite. I have heard more clapping at the worst of my plays. With an Indian audience you know where you stand.

The words were also few and formal. "We wish to thank Mr. Tagore for being with us today, for sharing his poetry and his time." Do they thank or do they wish to thank? I understand their language, but I do not understand the English.

My son and I walked afterwards on the heath with Mr. Rothenstein. William is a kind and welcoming man. You can see it in his art. He said not to bother. The English are not expressive, he explained. Their hearts are not given full reign. Perhaps they will come around.

I did not sleep well. Perhaps I insulted their language. How could I presume to be a poet in a language which is not mine? The translation was for myself only. How could I have allowed myself to be persuaded to stand before these men of letters, in the land of Shakespeare and Milton, reading my foolish words. I felt like a schoolboy.

And then the next day it started. A letter or two arrived, simple notes and cards really. "I did not know what to say." "Your words left me speechless." "It was an honour to be present in the room."

These English are another sort. To the face they cannot say, but with a pen in hand, they can express the feelings of their hearts. It is also the way of the writer, so I should understand. Sometimes I am the same.

Mr. Yeats says he reads my *Gitanjali* on the railway platform, upon the omnibus, at any spare moment, but quickly hides the book from view, lest some onlooker should see that he has been moved. Will they think less of him if they see a tear? Should they also not want that world?

Mr. Yeats has said the finest thing. My heart soars with his words. He calls my poetry a gift to English literature. He says *Gitanjali* is not simply an Indian voice, strange and far, but our voice. By "our voice" he mean the English, the Irish, the English-speaking world. He says I will be a bridge between East and West. What finer gift can I bear? It is all God's doing.

Yeats will edit this volume and is even himself writing an introduction. He will see to the publication. I made this trip to England for my health, for the sea air, a change of climate and a hope for treatment, but the truth is that it is for this book that my God has dragged me here at my age. It is literature and art and the like which are the real bridges uniting one country with another. I feel as if God is expressing His own gladness through others' praise of my work. It is as if He has brought me from East to West in order to make me aware of the fact of His gladness. His grace cannot be accepted in a state of infatuation, which is why I am preparing myself to submit to the honour with my forehead touching the dust.

Tagore's words haunted me. I returned to his statue many times, with and without Frieda. I even laid a garland of marigolds around his bronze neck and bowed in namaste. I read and reread his poems with deepening awe. A man of his stature with such piety, with such devotion was a model for my own life. He was a poet, a painter, a musician, a playwright, an essayist, an artist who was also an ambassador to the world. He was everything, but also wanted only to be a devotee of God.

The Nobel Prize came to him because of Yeats. They accepted his poems not as translations, but as originals composed in English. They honoured him because he honoured God. That was amazing. Europe was reaching out to India, prize in hand. India was reciprocating tenfold with an offering in song.

I tried in my life to be like Tagore: humble but confident, fearful and fearless, a visionary able to see and appreciate the smallest detail. To see the Creator in the the play of a child, to me that was Rabindranath Tagore. That is where I wanted to be.

Frieda shared my enthusiasm because it was my enthusiasm, my passion. She had planted it, but it was mine to cradle and kindle.

Tagore was a critic of education systems, heavy-handed schooling methods. He created an outdoor school of his own in Bengal. He believed that nature and art are the best teachers. Frieda and I dreamed of visiting that school. Thinking about it, we could feel the nurturing grace of the trees, the arid smoke, the spicy masala of earth and air. Dust mixed with wet paint. Frieda's art would flourish in such a place. Life and art and nature and God would all be one in such a place, not departments, separate drawers only opened one at a time.

Our plan was simple. Our money was enough to get us to London. In England, we would find a way to India, but it would be a step, a plateau upon which we could replenish. We would walk on Hampstead Heath where Tagore and Yeats had strolled together. We would see the vistas that inspired Wordsworth and Blake. Shakespeare would be our tutor.

We would find work and find a way. On this Earth, there are pockets of beauty. Each is different – a new beauty in each land, another colour on the palette of paints. These are refueling stations. Our quest, if we remained true, would take us where we needed to be.

We opened a new volume in our notebook with these words from the poet:

What is your quest, holding the lamp near your heart?

My house is all dark and lonesome – lend me your light.

5

all those other voices

Within us we have that
where space and time cease to rule
and where the links of evolution merge in unity.

Rabindranath Tagore

GALLERY

The first months in London were difficult. It was not what I was expecting. After the green rainforests of western Canada, I was back in the unwashed grime of a mega-city. History piled on history: castles next to garrisons, next to Roman walls, ancient battlefields, historic markers, fields of struggle now overbuilt with betting shops and pubs, history with every turn of the turf in the back garden.

I don't know what I was expecting to see, but there were glimmers, moments when the rays of auburn light broke through the thick clouds of inertia. The day I am remembering particularly is when Frieda took me to the Tate Gallery. It was a daylight-shortened winter's day, afternoon dimming to evening even before tea time.

As we climbed the broad stone steps, I felt a grounding heaviness, a gravity pulling at my bones. The gallery steps were the same grey as the sky. Both were as unfeeling as the other, immovable weights. I was beginning to feel that the whole of London was a deadweight, a bad decision.

Frieda, always attuned to my feelings, joys and sorrows both, was watching me. She was my barometer. She knew what was ahead.

"In most places, the skies are cobalt blue," she said. "Skies should be cobalt or azure, cream and berries, pie-in-the-sky puffy clouds, beautiful and rich, a wash, a wave from a palette or watercolour tray straight to a canvas or paper. But in London, the skies are stone slate grey. How do you paint that?" she asked. "Mix all the colours together and that's what you get: the grey skies of London. Orwell called it cobalt grey, a sky like a wall of dull grey stone."

I agreed, but I really wanted her to cheer me up.

"In Canada the skies were grey too, but I could paint that," she remembered. "There was a freshness in the air, a life and hope. Here there's only one way to do everything and it usually means standing in a queue." She was making things worse. "But wait until you see this," she added as we ascended to top of the stairs.

We bypassed the portraits, the temporary travelling exhibits, the modern art, the manicured landscapes, hunting dogs and children as displays of wealth. We stood at the entrance to a darkened room. The light was dimmed to protect the delicate watercolours, the fine print engravings, the illuminated pages. This was the William Blake exhibit hall.

"The finest things in London are indoors," Frieda explained, "and this is by far the finest I have found. I looked with interest and care. I had seen some of this before, but now I was looking with my eyes open. "One man painted all this?" I asked. And what was I doing with my life?

"One man like no other," Frieda replied.

I saw images from Shakespeare's plays, Paradise Lost, angels and demons, Old Testament and New, Adam and Eve, Jesus, his mother Mary, heavens and hells. His paintings were laced with poetry, waves of words and inspiration.

"He was an engraver," Frieda explained, "a printer, but also a poet and an artist. He took commissioned jobs to illustrate books and he took it all to a higher level. His poetry became a part of his pictures, so you can say he was everything: the author, the illustrator, the designer, the printer and the publisher all in the one man. He must have been a musician too. When I look at these paintings, I can feel the music."

I stopped and breathed the filtered air of the gallery. I felt the paintings, their light touching my face and skin. I looked at Frieda, her face close to a picture of angels with trumpets. Her eyes were closed.

I turned and walked back to the entrance. "Frieda," I whispered. I unlaced and removed my shoes and put them outside the gallery door.

"Frieda, we are in a temple."

I don't know how many times I returned to the Blake paintings during the time we lived in London. There were too many visits to count. Whenever I was passing, I dropped in. Whenever I needed, I made a special pilgrimage.

There is one painting among them all with which I became particularly fond. It was of the baby Jesus, a round-faced and radiant boy. Why didn't they show us this picture in school? I would have liked to have known this Jesus. He looked playful and wise and kind, while still being holy and divine. I stared at that portrait, returning to it again and again. Did a model sit in Mr. Blake's studio as he prepared and sketched? Or did the artist paint from his imagination? I decided it could only be a vision which brought this face to paper.

And then, as I was looking, I saw something I had never seen before. I actually stepped backwards with a feeling that something had shifted in the image, like an optical illusion, a change of perception. I looked. As the child Jesus sat on his mother's lap, the neckline of her dress was also the edge of a clear halo around his head. It was a part of the design, but so very subtle, so simple and natural.

Mr. Blake was many, many things. Above them all, he was also a visionary.

SURVEYS

In London I took a job. I met the people of that great city and within it of the nation, of the empire and the world. Completing surveys and questionnaires, public opinion polls, I knocked on their doors. I stood on their doorsteps, sometimes I was invited into their homes. Such people are these, I marvelled, able to carry on in the footsteps of their parents and ancestors. Such a sense of duty and value, fair play and sense of place. I felt that in recording their opinions, no matter how trite the subject, was to honour their fortitude.

I met people of all classes, walks, outlooks. Like a mosaic, one pebble at a time popped into colour, a full design slowly more visible with each interview, each question.

I asked about bus routes and utility services, about local government and national elections, hand soap preferences and football allegiances. These people, in Wandsworth council flats and Chelsea coach houses, in riverside townhouses and identically attached post-war row houses, one side of the street mirroring the other, they each took time with me. Some kept me at a respectful distance, chilled on their front step, rain dripping from above, the door ajar and secured by a foot. Others invited me inside for tea. They told me of their preferences on a scale from one to ten, their likelihood of voting, their television viewing, their income range, tastes, likes and dislikes. Then, with the survey complete, they poured a second cup and told me more.

In this way, many went beyond the printed questions. For them, the questionnaire was a starting point. I was interested and they were talking. The country was a mess and they knew how to fix it. I was making notes. Everything would be made right.

I grew to love these people. What had been a nation, a faceless crowd, became people, individuals. Hundreds stood before me. With each new face, my respect grew.

Then there was the day that I looked up from my clipboard to see something that at first delighted and then amazed. The English are a people who are prepared to be amazed. If something is not "brilliant," it is certainly "amazing."

In the mundane greyness of Lambeth, near the neck of the fanning rail line, as it approaches that great station Waterloo, I came upon the most modest block of flats, post-war, rebuilt in the wake of blitz-bombing, modern with right angles and thin-framed windows – and with one pop of colour, a blue plaque commemoration. "William Blake Poet & Painter Lived in a house formerly on this site 1793." Around a corner, on an entrance wall, the tiles of a mosaic crudely simulated one of Blake's watercolours. While his paintings were fluid and delicate, flowing with a unity, this mosaic was at first a scattergun of confusion. It was a replica only, nothing without the original.

But then, as my thoughts went away, as I remembered Mr. Blake and thought of his determined steps on this same Hercules Road, I slowly felt a tide of beauty, a magic in this raw rendition.

Each blue or green or yellow tile alone was nothing, but together they were like a single being, humanity, an Albion rising.

Blake, once on this now so-changed road, hurrying out in hopes of a commission or a promise, returning home in disappointment, disillusioned, must have looked at that heaven-pointing spire of Christ Church, still today standing, considering what mess men make of religion, of spirit, of the gifts of this Earth, how they re-shape the image of God to serve their own needs, they cap their dreams, limit themselves and see nothing.

I continued to stand. It was in complete amazement I stood. The grey, dull day, in this clockwork city, knew nothing of the spirit, nothing of rebirth or renewal. Yet through the nearly two centuries of time, I could feel the poet Blake on this spot. I could feel the painter Blake surveying this street with an unblinkered vision. I could feel the engraver Blake, the Englishman, the free-thinker, the visionary and saint. There was no need to run to the Tate Temple, no need to remove my shoes in veneration or bow my head in obeisance. I stood now with perfect vision, shackles and filters released in a single clattering crash to the ground. The unity of all humans in one body was something I had long known. But now, I also felt it.

It was not an understanding that comes from the mind, not a brain ticking to a calculated conclusion. It was a knowledge that alights as a bird nesting on a branch.

The nightingale had arrived. I was amazed. And I was ready.

SQUATTER

You would think with so many people, so many doors and faces, that they would all blend into one or else be forgotten entirely in the fog of years. But still, I remember.

Individual tiles in that mosaic stand out. They are short exposure photos, to be sure, moments in the lives of real people, but I can recall them now like so many snapshots tacked to a corkboard wall, like hundreds of reminders indexed on cards, colour-coded and filed.

I pull one out now: a woman in Islington. She is a career actress. Another: a pensioner forgotten in a pre-war council flat. "I lived through the blitz, love, I think I can manage a leaky tap." A single mother with two children. A Polish immigrant in Twickenham. A newlywed couple in Hounslow, so optimistic, so naive.

What is it that makes people all so different and also the same? At the core there is a spark, a flame that maintains and guides, a feeling – sometimes ignored, sometimes vague, but always there – a hope that is held that it is all for something, some reason, some greater purpose. How do they manage to pull through?

There was a man. I remember. He was a squatter I assumed. It was not his own house. He never said. I only guessed.

By some archaic law, he could stay unharassed because he had found the building vacant. It was the squatter's right. There was gas, but it came from portable refillable tanks. There was light, but it came from candles and handheld flashlights. The heat was from coal in an open fireplace. The house was not his, but he had made it his own. With a hole punched through a central wall and painted around with colours and spirals, celestial images, Spidermen, commercial mascots and logos, a drunk Mickey Mouse, flags and vulgarity, an anarchist A, a dollar sign and Nazi swastika, he had personalized it all to an extreme. Distress and division filled every surface, but also paint and colour, art and anger. It was a celebration, but also an exploded shrapnel-filled landmine.

It was as if all the colour and filth had spilled from that hole or maybe it was being sucked into it, slowly draining, disappearing into a black hole. It was not his house, but his art had made it his. The house was his art. And why not?

He was an older man, but hard to gauge. His quick movements suggested someone younger. His radical ideas were rooted somewhere, in some anger, some injustice. He was a rebel. Art was his weapon of choice.

His hands were stained with paint and tobacco. His chin was not a yuppie stubble, but an anarchist's "I don't care." His language was laced with profanities scattered like chicken feed across the room, like darts missing the board, biting the skin, random. Everything was an irritation, a capitalist scab, a plot against the people.

Still, this squatter, this man, this spirit within a body, sat with me. He laid aside his brushes, first mopping them with a turpentine rag, laying them side by side, parallel, shortest to longest. He found me a chair, poured tea from a Brown Betty pot and opened a fresh box of Peek Freans. "I'll be mother, shall I?" he said. His smile was mischievous, but also sweet and genuine. He knew I wasn't the enemy.

That man told me so much. I put down my clipboard and just listened. Was I there twenty minutes, a half an hour, an hour? Eclectic, self-educated, drawing from everywhere, making connections, he told me plenty – whatever popped into his head, unfiltered. He filled and refilled my brain with ideas as rapidly as he refilled my teacup. Conspiracies and paranoias, the paranormal and the obvious-to-anyone.

"Everything is connected," he said. "We're all serving somebody. And if it's not yourself, you better know who it is. The Man doesn't care and can spit you out and replace you with another. Put that on your public opinion survey."

"I think that would be a ten, then," I replied, "on a scale of one to ten."

"Eleven at least," he laughed. "It's all a myth – everything, come the revolution."

And from it all, there is one thing I remember most clearly. We were standing at the door. I was zipping my jacket, preparing to leave. It is as if he said to me, "If when we part, you remember nothing else, my friend, remember this…."

But this is what he actually said: "Optimism is the thing."

I was taken aback. It didn't fit into the diatribe that I had just witnessed, this footnote, asterisked and then circled in red. I wanted to say, "How's that? So simple?"

He didn't wait for a question. He kept on. "When you get to my age," – he glanced up and down the street checking for onlookers, conspirators, the constabulary – "and you look at the young, it's not their health that you will envy. It's not their good looks, rosy cheeks, their nice head of hair. It's their optimism. That's the thing: optimism. Knowledge is nothing. Wisdom is nothing. It's optimism that is the fuel for life. It's the only thing that will get you across, from one side to the other."

I pulled my gloves tight, preparing to leave.

"Optimism is believing. You have to believe that there has to be a good reason for all this." He waved his arm, taking in everything – the houses, the street, the distant train always rattling out of sight, the city, the world. "Cheers, mate," he added with a quick salute. "Salutations to the people."

When he said "mate," I really felt he meant it.

OFFICE

There are moments when time stops. Perception changes. You are in the flow of life, a river of currents, eddies, backwaters, battling, manoeuvring. Then you are above it, looking down, no longer back paddling, no longer a player. No anxiety, no questioning, you are a witness, simply watching, uninvolved.

I stood in my boss' office, alone. I could have been dropped there like a time traveller, one moment a boy playing cricket in Nargol, the next an employee at a market research firm on a suburban edge London. India to England, child to married man – if you had asked me in that moment, I would not have been able to connect one point to the other.

My boss – they called a director on his business card – was a man who was himself bossed. Through a long string of command, a ladder of duties, responsibility and function, he also answered to others. As I waited, he had gone for instructions, to get a report, more papers and numbers. He had been vague, but he had told me to wait. The result: I was alone.

In a company where something was always happening – ringing phones, rushed footsteps, the clatter and chatter of keyboards and hushed gossip, interruptions on all sides – this room was a calm escape, a time-out. I was removed, floating above it all.

I looked out the window. My eyes unfocused, gazed across the car park – yellow lines on smooth blacktop, cars in varying hues of grey and grey-blue, aligned and rowed, ordered, ranked by their closeness to the building. Hashed and hazmat warnings: max headroom, no standing.

The outside was a dull as the office: grey carpet, beige curtains, dim lamps, corporate art on corporate walls, drab and uninspired.

How had I come to be here? I knew. The ships and planes, the cars and simple decisions of my life could all be accounted for. A to B, then to C, not D. I could map it out, graph it. The line of a life contains a logic, but what of the guiding hand of God and His guardian angels? What of destiny? Did a simple decision like boarding the *Marathi Pride* or a piece of luck like meeting Rusty land me in this spot, in this place and moment rather than somewhere else? Without the *Pride*, there would have been no Sharma. Without Sharma, there would have been no Rupert. And without Rupert, no Rusty, no Mrs. Freeman. And no Frieda.

My life was a string of pearls or a line of falling dominos, take your pick. One mis-step and I could now be standing in a market stall in Dar es Salam or a carnival kiosk in Mexico. My head hurt with the thoughts. "So far, so good," I whispered to myself, "but help me navigate what is to come."

I turned. I did what I had done so often in my life. I made an inventory. As if this was my father's shop, I counted the stock on hand. Three pencils, aligned and sharp. One paperweight, ugly. An in-box, an out-box, one above the other. One telephone. A line of business cards tacked to a cork board with neat precision. Pushpins, all black. Predictable and routine. Dull.

A notepad was centred on the desk blotter, more business cards and preprinted "while you were out" notes tucked along the side, urgent checkmarked on every one. The notepad was yellow. The blue lines could not contain the sprawling words, soft pencil lead on even softer paper. A letter-opener. Letters, torn by hand, hastily opened. A waste bin. A paper shredder.

I moved to the small side couch. I sat. Comfortable, but not meant for a long stay. An array of business magazines, annual reports, restaurant menus across the low table. A newspaper half-covered a flare of colour: orange and red on stark, pure white. It was an explosion, a bright celebration on a field of grey newsprint and corporate blues. My head tilted, leading my shoulder and then my hand. I eased myself forward, kneeling on the floor before the table, moving forward to see more.

There was a spiral, a spin, deep confident brush strokes. I pulled back the newspaper. The red and orange lead to quick splashes of pinks and greens. How long had it been since I had seen this? It was Shri Ganesha, elephant head on a child's body, wisdom and innocence together. Not in Vancouver or Rupert, maybe on the *Marathi Pride*, but there as a good luck charm, a mascot, not a lord or protector, not a deity. He was probably at the gate of the Nargol beach temple, certainly in My father's store, up high, looking down beside Sai Baba and Shri Krishna, a dried and faded garland around the framed and equally faded print, a spent incense stick in the cracks of the plaster wall. The saints and deities oversaw all trade in our tiny store. Their presence in the form of mass produced prints was our blessing, priced to move.

I looked. Like seeing an old friend, I reached my hand forward in recognition. Like seeing a deity, my movement was with obeisance and service. The picture of Shri Ganesh was bright and bold across the cover of the neatly bound book. It was a catalogue, a program or a souvenir from an art exhibit. It was placed on the table, a diversion for waiting guests, but for me an inspiration.

My hand touched the cover with reverence. Curious, thoughtless, I wanted more of this art, this beauty, this memory of home. Like a rising wave from the deep of the ocean, it overtook and carried me, a swelling current, a rising tide. I took a corner with both hands. I opened the book.

Sometimes we rush, breakfast in one hand, keys in the other. Sometimes we wait, "when will life move, when will I have change?" But then, there are moments when time is ours to savour and hold. The moment expands and reveals. Time stands to one side. She is the servant to truth.

I opened the book. Some things happen even before they happen. I knew what I would see. I could feel the invitation.

The art displayed on the inner pages showed a side of India I had never seen: modern, interpretive, bright and fresh, but also devotional and pure, traditional and eternal. It was modern art, but it was timeless. Krishna was the charioteer. Hanuman flew to Lanka, tail aflame. I turned the pages. Lakshmi balanced impossibly on a floating lotus. Again Shri Ganesha, rope in one hand, a goad in the other, simultaneously moving us forward and holding us back. With a third hand, he was blessing. In the fourth, he held a coconut.

I remembered the coconut floating from my hands on the waters of Hecate Strait on that first day in Rupert, bobbing like a fishing float, auspicious and beautiful. I closed my eyes with the thought. The memory came and went. I was in that moment.

Then the next page turned. It held a red ribbon, placed to mark. The ribbon was looped and tied to a card, a bookmark. On it was the face of a woman, serene and beautiful, a mother, but more. Beneath were the words, "A primordial force rising like a telescope opening out, a torrential rain flowing."

There was more, but I stopped. Frozen. Something gripped me. It was not a fear. It was the opposite. It was awe. If I could have dived into the book, hidden behind Shri Ganesha's dancing foot, taken refuge in Krishna's chariot, I would have. How had I come to be here, in this moment, in this room? I was a boy again, seeing a strange world of office furniture, company politics, vanity and mistrust. But this world, this book, this art was my world – the card, the words and especially the photo.

When my boss returned, I could not tell how much time had passed. My mind was emptied. It was emptied to make room for only one thought, a single question: what now?

He spoke to me, shuffled papers, pointed. His finger ran the slopes, the rise and falls of graph lines. He turned pages and circled words with ballpoint ink. He clicked the pen nervously. He asked me if I understood. I heard nothing. I said yes.

HOMEWARD

As I rode the train home that evening, my mind had again become a crowded circle of thoughts.

I had taken that job for money alone. It was a simple and straightforward transaction: labour for pounds, money for travel. We would get to India one day distant. Market research, public opinion, consumer feedback, focus groups. I went from door to door asking questions, checking boxes, listening and noting. I did the same on the telephone: "On a scale from one to ten, how would you rate ... Tesco Tea, your local bus service, the power authority, Wheatabix, the Labour Party? Excellent, very good, good, somewhat good...?" From street and phone, I moved to an office desk, processing the data, correlating, reporting, a great deal of nothing. And then back to the streets again. And all to what end?

From the rail carriage I watched. I saw the blur of back gardens, the bricked walls, drainpipes, chimney pots, kitchen windows, brief glimpses into other lives. The train rattling, but never knowing.

I contemplated my job and the lives of others, but, in all that, I was avoiding the core of my concern. I looked down to my hand. I held the ribboned photo, the marker from the art book. I had asked and he had given.

"I don't know who she is," he said. "Someone gave it to me at the show. He was passing them out. He might have been one of the artists or someone's friend. I don't know. I put it in the book. It seemed like a good place. Her face is kind. It didn't seem right to throw it out."

I don't know what I said to him or what kind of look I had. Mostly, I was just looking at the woman in the photo the entire time. "You can have it if you want," he said. It was really only a card and a ribbon like hundreds of photographs or postcards that come to us in a lifetime. Most of them are memorabilia, souvenirs mass-produced. A few are cherished and tucked away and then forgotten. But mostly they are briefly regarded and then quickly discarded.

But this man could see. He could see I was taken. "Know thyself it says on the back," he said. "That's good advice."

To the core of my bones, to the fibre of my being, to the heart of my soul, as I travelled homeward on that train, I knew this was the woman I had seen on the Nargol beach. I couldn't prove it with words or facts, but the face and the serenity spoke to my heart. "Know thyself" spoke to my mind. And the words "a torrential rain flowing" spoke to my spirit.

In my memory, there was a recognition, a boy calling out to me from long ago.

As the evening darkened and the interior carriage lights came on, I could see my reflection in window of the train. I shifted slightly in my seat, somehow trying to see around myself, my reflected image. The houses and shops and streets were left to right a constant unrolling, a scroll of images the same every day. My face, my head and shoulders, in reflection were layered on top. I watched myself watching.

I reached towards the window. The train braked and slowed. A station fence, a sign, a platform, then people, waiting passengers. I did not divert my eyes this time. I stared at myself and stared again. Perhaps he would look away first.

"Not the reflection," I thought. "I want the real thing."

POSTERS

As many times as I had visited the Tate, taking refuge in that temple, I think Frieda was also making regular attendance or was otherwise garnering pure inspiration from the artist. You could see it in her paintings.

From lilacs and larks, simple flowery embroidery, Frieda's art rose to the heavens. The larks became angels, the flowers exploded, radiant and transcendent. Rather than objects of the world, Frieda's brush created qualities, the forces and flows that were stellar: innocence and wisdom, love and forgiveness. She was no longer interested in reflecting the world. She wanted to prophesy what could be, the truth beneath the mundane, not what-if, but what-will.

A flower was no longer a flower in Frieda's eye. As she feathered the edges, it became hope. A bird in flight, flushed out by her brush, became ascension. The Earth was a nurturing mother. And one child was all of humanity.

Her art reached. And it was embraced. Slowly it also gained an audience.

The task of putting up Frieda's posters was a pleasure on many levels. I was helping her, that was certain, but I was also was able to walk the streets of London, not as a tourist, not just to complete a survey, but with a mission.

The posters were vibrant. They are her art. They were her. They expressed heartfelt wonder while at the same time advertising causes and concern: "Nuclear Free Britain If You Want It." "Save the Whales. Save Yourself." "One Earth One People." The messages were simple. "Start here. Start now." Sometimes the posters advertised rallies, protests or parades. Sometimes they acted as a call for donations, a vote in an election or the mobilization of opinion and awareness. Sometimes the posters were commissioned and she received a small fee. Sometimes they were her own initiative: art for the people, an expression of love, like sweet graffiti in full colour. The thing was that her art was so good, so fresh and original that the posters were often stolen. Frieda didn't seem to mind. "On the street or in the sitting room, doesn't matter, people still see it."

And there was a sweet bonus: there were a few bookstores, poster shops, record stores and even restaurants that would take the posters and resell them. At first it was on a consignment basis. Later, as Frieda's reputation grew, they were asking for the posters framed, signed and numbered. There was a gallery in Soho which often featured her art in the window. It brought people into the shop, they said, a wide range of customers.

What had started as activism and personal heartfelt expression grew into a small movement. We called it the Art of Joy and other artists, friends with the same vision, joined in.

So it was both a joy and it was a job. It also took my attention away from all the worries, pestering thoughts and confusions. Our sights were still set on India, but the money, even with all of Frieda's accidental success, was coming slowly.

London, like so many big cities, is a place of disconnection. Like burrowing groundhogs, people disappear into holes, ride a train and then emerge miles away, never quite knowing how the two places fit together. In London, Kew Gardens, Trafalgar Square, Marble Arch and Knightsbridge were like rotating satellites without fixed orbits. The Underground map, stylized with straightened coloured lines, was little help. The reality of distance, the subtle shadings of neighbourhoods, the snaking of the Thames could only be understood by walking. So that is what I did.

With a shoulder roll of posters, I walked, putting up Frieda's art, depositing her leaflets, recording in my small notepad the wheres and whens, the positioning of each. From Putney to White City, Kensington, Hampstead, Edgeware Road and onward, I stepped, tacked, pasted and repeated. I told myself I was decorating the city, making London a beautiful place again.

Frieda's posters were beautifully wonderous displays, multi-coloured washes, artistry that made people smile. One World, Gaia, Mother Earth – these were her concerns. Her posters were works of art, created to dazzle, fresh and alive. A tortoise carried a mass of land on the curve of its back. Birds circled, supporting a clean and vibrant dome of sky. Like a new Noah, her posters were arks for all of God's creatures. I was honoured to place these images in shops, libraries, recreation centres, wherever they were accepted. And because of their beauty, acceptance came easy. People love beauty.

ONE POSTER

I was at Waterloo Station. It was often a starting point, that hub of activity and travel. I loved the mix of people from city workers finely dressed to trainspotters with clipboards and sun visors. New arrivals, tourists and immigrants and there I was, Vishesh Darshane, standing before the arrivals and departures board watching the clicking cascade of letters and numbers.

Central London was an impossible land for postering. Clean shops with even cleaner, maintained windows were the norm, pubs with ornamental small-paned windows alongside windowless betting shops. I decided to walk south and west towards Wandsworth and perhaps Clapham. For handbills and posters, it was friendlier territory than crossing to the north side of the river. The people might also offer me a gentler welcome.

It was warm and lovely, a rare full summer day. The shops – hairdressers, small grocers, even doner kebab shops took Frieda's posters with interest, even enthusiasm. But I hit the jackpot when I came upon a large new and used bookshop. Here was a community board rich with space reserved, the sign said, "for non-commercial, progressive, community-oriented, cultural, not-for-profit causes – for the people."

I looked at Frieda's poster as I held it measuring it against the board. It seemed to fit in every category and description. I pulled out my staple gun and surveyed the board. Where to put it? The space was large, but entirely covered: community garden, free performance, open mic, rally, parade, poetry reading – it was all there. I began to read. "Speaking tonight only." That could go. It wasn't today's tonight. I peeled the poster back. Many of the advertisements had expired. The events had come and gone. The date had passed and then some. Many were more than a month old.

I began to clear and then widen a space. I dug and tore with increased vigour. I reached down like an archaeologist moving back through time, the early summer just past, then into the spring months. The layers of weather-stiffened paper was thick. I was determined. This was prime territory and I was beautifying the city, even the world.

I pulled out a knife and began to work at the rusted staples, the pushpins and thumb tacks. I cut with the blade until a full section of encrusted paper fell away like a side of a mountain or section of glacier.

I stopped. What I saw made me. Preserved beneath the layers was a full colour photograph glued to a deep red, full-size sheet poster. It was an Indian woman. It was the same woman I had seen on the bookmark.

My mind swam. I was riveted. Beneath the photo were the words: "Know Thyself." I removed more paper and debris. And below that: "Caxton Hall. St. James Park SW1. Mondays 6 pm."

With my knife, I carefully cut and sawed the poster free. I placed it in my bag, careful to keep it right side up. It was protected between the others.

It was a good distance, but I walked without stopping, without thinking, towards Battersea Park, crossing the Thames at Chelsea Bridge, the iconic power station behind me and then onwards to Westminster.

CAXTON HALL

Anywhere else, Caxton Hall would be an imposing Victorian structure. But in central London, so close to Buckingham Palace and St. James Park and the gentlemen's clubs of Pall Mall, it was simply one of many – another red brick, fanciful and ornate facade, a splendour from another time. In India, or even in Canada, we would have called it colonial, but this was no colony. This was where it all started, the base of the power.

As I approached the hall, this wandering thought was confirmed. A blue plaque fixed prominently to an exterior wall declared as much: "Sir Winston Churchill spoke here 1937 - 1942." That was a long speech, I thought. He must have had a lot to say. I smiled to myself. What if Indians commemorated their history in this same way. There would be plaques everywhere.

I hurried up the steps. It looked like the hall might be closing. The door propped open by a wooden wedge was being shut by an employee. He wore a suggestion of a uniform, a square-fitting jacket with a name tag, a clipboard, book and pen in his hand. He kicked the wedge with his foot, trying to dislodge it as he looked towards me. "Evening, sir," he said as I passed inside.

The entrance was grand, but aged, worn by the years, like a cinema palace, but without the light veneer of entertainment. This was a venue for great speakers and serious topics. I stared at the wood paneling, the curve of the staircase. I don't know what I was expecting to see.

I turned back towards the man at the door. "Have you come for the function?" he asked.

"I'm looking," I said. I reached for the poster in my bag, drawing it out and showing him, "for this." I felt I should have said "her" or "this woman," but still he understood.

"Oh, a bit late then. That all finished years ago. I was thinking you'd come for the geology meet. A lot of things happen here, great and small. They all come and go. Different people, different ideas. We've had a lot. Today it's rocks."

"I see" was all I could say.

"You've come a long way then?"

"Yes and no. My name is Vishesh. I'm just a traveller, kind of a tourist."

He looked at me. "I dare say if you are from India, you could probably find her there. More likely there than any other place."

I paused. There was a lot of ways I could go with this, a lot I could say in reply. My story wasn't so simple.

"Maybe you're interested in history," he said. I could see by his name tag that his name was Gilles. He saw me looking at the name. "You can call me Derek." He offered his hand for shaking. With the other, he gave me a pamphlet, a simple piece of paper folded twice, text with photos. "Something I made myself," he added. "I've been here a while. They let me tinker some."

Caxton Hall – a short history. I scanned the words, feigning interest, nodding my head. Built 1842. Westminster Town Hall. Winston Churchill. Suffragettes, a women's parliament. Protests. Labour rallies. Assassination, governor of Punjab, Caxton Hall. Six bullets fired.

"We had marriages here until '79," he said sweetening the story, "being a town hall and registry office. Elizabeth Taylor, Ringo Starr, one of the Bee Gees I think, married between these walls, confetti on the steps I suppose. People are more interested in that sort of history.

I smiled, still reading: Ragindranath Tagore. "Tagore was here?" I asked.

"Tagoremania. You know Tagore then?" Derek asked. "It was before the first war. He was all the rage in London, reading his poems, giving speeches, the universal Self, the brotherhood of man, love and peace, the whole thing. There weren't a lot of Indians around, was before the immigration wave. Someone like you would have been very exotic indeed, but probably not trusted as far as you could throw a turban. But Tagore fit the bill exactly, tall and stately, foreign, but wise. I've seen the photos. That whole Eastern thing started with him. People loved it."

This Derek didn't seem like an educated man, but then neither was I in those days, but he spoke with the confidence of a man standing in his own front garden. He knew all about this hall. "It's named after the inventor of the printing press. That says it all right there, doesn't it – first thing, communication.

"Tagore talked here two, three times at most, but that woman you got on that poster, she was here plenty more. A hundred times maybe, every week, on and off over a few years."

"You saw her?" I asked.

"I stood at the back. It was my job to check in and see that everything was all right, enough chairs, that kind of thing. Then when I came to know she'd be there, I made it a point."

"How do you mean?"

"I got interested. At first, I didn't get it. I mean there was a lot of talking, like a lecture, like school, then there was just silence, eyes closed. The next week it was the same. Mostly the same people back again."

"And...."

"And then I listened and stopped thinking about it. She had a way for sure. She talked about love. But I'd heard that before. Remember, Ringo and George had both been here. Fame and celebrity were not on my shopping list. But this Mataji, she talked about the time for blossoms and totality, being one, connection. That caught my attention. I'm always interested in connecting things, the present to the past, people to each other. It wasn't like she was pitching a cause or looking for members, I don't think, not recruiting like some. Your mother doesn't try to sell you anything, does she? It was like that.

"One time I took a chair near the back, just decided to sit down like everyone else. I listened. People were coming in, a few were leaving, wasn't for them I guess, but I listened. Slowly, slowly, it started to make sense. People don't often talk about the big picture, why we are here, the purpose of living. We avoid that, the English, but she took it head-on.

"Then she said for everyone new to move up to the front. There were lots of seats in the hall. The people were scattered all over. She said new people, first-time-comers should sit in the front rows. At first, I thought I'm working, I should keep moving. Then I thought to hell with it. I took off my jacket, left it on a back chair and moved to a front seat.

"Like that it happened. I can't speak about exactly what happened to me. It's way beyond words."

"The moment is everything," I said.

"Yes. Like that. And a coolness, a wind but not a wind."

"I know," I said.

"I figure we only usually use a little bit of our senses and too much of our brain. When I was there in front of her, I was feeling a lot. My senses were working fully for the first time."

"Enlightened." I wasn't filling in words for him, but understanding and agreeing.

"Enlightened. That's what they mean when they say that: like the light has been switched on. But, you know, the truth is I didn't feel enlightened. I felt like a little boy." He was silent, remembering.

"She talked to me a bit. She asked me if I could feel it. I said yes. She said that's good. I said I worked in the Hall and needed to get back. Her eyes were very large. She said it was a good place to work and she laughed and smiled at me. I'll always remember that. The thing is this: I felt like a boy, a little boy with the world alight with wonder and sparkle. Have you ever felt that?"

"Once or twice."

"I hope I haven't said too much. I just like telling that story and when you showed me her picture on the poster, it all came back. Sometimes I feel she's here. If you are calm inside you can feel it too. All those other voices have faded, but I remember her."

I was silent. I imagined all the people who had ever been in that Caxton Hall, at the entrance, climbing the stairs, finding their seats. Chamberlain and Churchill, the suffragettes and agitators, the visionaries. Tagore and this holy mother, this Mataji.

"They would have had a lot to talk about, Mataji and Tagore," Derek said. "I wonder if they ever met. It's possible you know, quite possible."

I paused to consider the conversation.

"You know, they called her Mother. That seems to fit. It says it all."

STEPS

I stayed near Caxton Hall very late that night. It was warm. I sat on the stone of front step of the closed hall. The geologists were gone, their last conversations about rocks and minerals and dinner and drinks faded down the street towards the St. Ermin's Hotel.

I felt like I was in India. I had not had that feeling for a long time. Perhaps it was the sun-warmed step upon which I sat, perhaps it was my thoughts of Mataji and Tagore. I could taste the chai, the pakora, the late evening street snacks of my younger days.

My thoughts trailed towards my school friends still there, my family, my parents, Patel and Sat. Was it true my sister Jagruti was now married? I needed to be in India again. As Derek had said, "there more than any place."

As it grew darker, I remembered the late evenings in India. I imagined the cows moving down Caxton Street, their feet raising a fine dust, their homeward journey. I could see them rounding the corner, some with large discordant bells, others swaying, timeless in their step.

Later, when I reached home, Frieda greeted me at the door. In her kindness, she always waited for my return. She spoke to me softly. "Your sister wrote. She said your father is asking for you. They don't think he is going to die, but maybe. He is asking for you to run for some Neem."

I smiled slightly.

"What is this Neem, Vishesh? Can we get some?"

"It can be done."

you have come a long way

My house is small
and what once has gone from it can never be regained.
But infinite is thy mansion, my lord,
and seeking her I have to come to thy door....
On the seashore of endless worlds is the great meeting of children.

Rabindranath Tagore

BOMBAY

When necessity calls, we always somehow find a way.

Frieda told me to go ahead. She said she would follow. She said my place was with my father and family. She handed me a small box. Along with gifts for my brothers and sisters and parents, there was a neatly tied cloth-covered package. It was the current volume of our notebook. "Take it with you," she said. "There are still many pages to fill." With Frieda, I never felt unloved, even in our parting.

In India, I saw my family. They were mostly unchanged. My father was older, but not as sick as I had feared. At first I questioned whether he knew who I was. His mind seemed to wander. His attention was short. Then I thought he was remembering another son as he spoke – Ravindra, but more likely Adi. Then he said, out of nowhere, "Quick, Vishesh, run quick. Customer needs some Neem. Run!" Then he laughed and laughed. He knew it was a joke. He was laughing because I was unsure.

.

India had changed. It all seemed different. But then I realized the changes were all superficial like a new coat of paint. Change happens, but India endures. I was the one who had changed. I was so young when I walked aboard the *Marathi Pride*. I knew nothing – nothing of the sea, the world beyond, the way people do things and then justify their actions in their own minds. Ignorance can be a curse, but innocence is also a protection. And a blessing.

Now, so many years later, I still knew nothing. But now, I was also aware of the extent of my ignorance, the limits of my knowledge.

The first thing I noticed in India was the heat. It hit me like a blast when the plane door swung open, breaking our seal to the outside world. The heat was unbearable, deadening, not fit for humans. Can you imagine? I had become so acclimatized to the temperate north that I was no longer an Indian in that respect. Had I softened to the nurturing touch of the sun. I felt both faint and weakened, suddenly zapped of any ambition or direction.

I also noticed the crowds. People are everywhere in India. Canada had been the land of self service – pump your own gas, find your own shoes. The corner of England I had known was a land of no service – shuttered shops, merchants in hiding, closed doors or, at best, limited hours.

In India, one transaction demands a minimum of five pairs of hands: a clerk, a wrapper, a cashier, an apprentice and a manager each with a task and an opinion. This is topped off by five to ten observers, men with nothing to do but watch. No need for security cameras here. Everything is watched, passively judged and approved or condemned.

Yes, I had changed. India was much the same. Invasion after invasion can sweep across this land, from the Moguls to the British, like the tide rising and receding. Still India abides. Unchanged, she carries on like a village woman returning from the well, the pot balanced on her head, not a drop is spilled. She is unconcerned because she knows that she carries a truth that cannot be broken, diluted or stolen away on a galloping horse.

I stand now watching like an observer, like all the others, men and boys patient before the pageant, a tableau that repeats and unfolds in endless variation of the same story. We all know the story. It is the retelling that gives cheer to our hearts.

In Bombay I had hoped to see Patel. He was my only link to that other world. I followed every lead from the Aurora Cinema to Marut Road. I had forgotten the names, but when I saw the old marquee and the street signs, I remembered. Every possible person, I asked, until I gave up. "He must be long gone," I thought. "He was very old."

I am an outsider, no longer a participant, no longer a stakeholder. Who am I in this ebb and flow? I feel myself stepping back and then back again in half steps of hesitation. I am no longer a boy dodging a cricket ball. I am now a married man, a traveller, a consumer, a citizen of somewhere else. The list goes on. But I know nothing of the moves I should make, the gestures that give meaning, the nuances that add to my performance.

I am an actor on this stage, but a sudden amnesia has caught me. My lines, so carefully memorized, have evaporated. Where is the prompter to whisper in my ear? Can I ad lib and still maintain the illusion? What is my cue? What is the title of this play? It seems that everyone knows but me.

In a long ago India, I was once a boy, one among millions. I have seen the world, now I again stand on a Bombay street. I feel ever smaller, now not one among millions, but one man among billions. Life has a way of telling you that you are special and then laughing and telling you that you are not. What am I to believe?

I am faint. When I fall it is not all at once, not a collapse or a tumble. Like a puppet, one string severed, then another. First my forearm, then a leg, lifeless, without suspension. My master is no longer the puppeteer. Now it is gravity. I fall.

How long has it been? The pavement is pressed to my cheek and temple. There is a smell, a coarseness. I am helped to a chair, perhaps it is a small wall or a rock. Warm water. To my face and mouth. The street is tilting still. Cars push up an impossible slope. People step downward. The sun is too much. I am gone again.

CHAI

I sit. It is evening. I am at a streetside chaiwallah, a single chair at a single table. I am the only customer. Both table and chair wobble, unstable. Maybe it is me.

The ground at my feet is red clay, hardened dust, caked and sloped by long ago rains. It is still hot, radiating from the day's sun. So am I.

The notebook is before me on the table. It is open, but I am unable to write. No words, no wisdom. I take up the pencil and draw:

soft billowing clouds, lines of light and rain, a sun and stars together in one sky.

I cradle a clay cup between my hands. I think of my father, now bedridden, so far away. The cup warms my hands as it did for my father, but does little for my heat-induced headache. The city is cooling, slowly surrendering to the night. I am feeling a little more myself, but also with the same slowness. There is a numbness, a humming in my head like a pestering mosquito, like a refrigerator labouring without coolant, a steady complaint from within.

My father took solace from his chai. The cup gave him comfort and wellbeing. I try, but I seem to be swimming backwards. My efforts work against me. I know I will feel better, but there is little hint of it happening yet.

I close my eyes in resignation, a surrender to whatever might be. Who am I to chart the course? I never was a real navigator.

I give up. The moment I surrender, I hear his voice: "I heard you were looking," he says from somewhere behind and from above. "For me, Vishesh, I heard you were looking."

I open my eyes. Is it the end of a long day or is it already the beginning of the next? He stands over me with a smile. "Are we having eggs today?" he asks.

Patel is here. I can hardly believe.

"You asked for me in all the right places, but you forgot. Ambika, not Patel. Still, I got your message. The ganas assist when God's work is to be done."

After some time, after some pieces of conversation that lead nowhere, he comes to the point, "Vishesh, you found me. But are you still looking?"

"For her," I said.

"They are here now."

"In Bombay?"

"Yes. She is here. And many others, from all the countries, foreigners, Indians. They will go down the coast soon. She will go also. There is a chance."

I was silent for a long time. It was neither hesitation or delay. Still, Patel waited, patient.

I looked at him, this man from my boyhood, my friend and guide. "I would like," I said, "if it is not too late."

Together we leave. Stepping tentatively at first, I have regained some of my strength. We move down the road in silence. There is nothing more to say. I do not seek advice. After all these years, there is no need. Patel has given direction. Advice is not needed.

Then I stop. The notebook is not with me. I turn and look back. The people, the traffic, even at this hour are like a barrier, a wavering curtain between me and the book. In the distance the chai stand is still there. I think of the notebook, open on the small table, the pencil to one side. Maybe they are gone, cleared away or stolen. Maybe they are collected, secure, awaiting my return.

I pause. Patel is quiet, unquestioning. I think of Frieda. The notebook. It is no longer needed. We turn again, continuing on our way.

DIRECTIONS

It has happened hundreds of times. A man stops you on the street. He asks directions. "Can you tell me how to find?" He might have a description or he might have a piece of paper with an address. You look at him or you look at the paper. You point and you might say, "Go to the top of the street and turn left" or "You are very close, almost there, keep to the right, watch for the red awning, you can't miss it." You part. The man is happy in the reassurance that he is on course. You are happy to have been there to help. You never meet again.

Now there is GPS, mapping and tracking, talking computers that you hold in your hand. All this is done for you. It knows where you are. You tell it where you want to go. It walks you through the route. "Turn left 400 meters." There is no need to ask. For all the convenience gained, human contact is lost.

I stood on the street in Bombay. The people flowed in all directions. They know where they are going, assured in the knowledge that there is a place for each of them and exactly, precisely they know how to get there.

Should I ask? Should I follow? Left or right, does it matter? It is the lunch hour and it is hot. I know one thing: I cannot stay here. I will bake and fry. I am not a mad dog.

I clear my mind. I empty my thoughts. "Go away," I tell my brain. "Later I will deal with your pestering questions."

I know what to do. I study the faces of the pedestrians. I look for a man of some years. He should be alone. Glasses would be good. Not in too much of a hurry, educated. I see him. This is the man. I step forward. I address him in English. "Sir," I say, "can you tell me where to find a bookshop? English language. Spiritual books, sacred texts."

He looks at me and begins to speak. "Yes, yes," as much as to say, "Do not leave me, I will have your answer as soon as I gather together my information, as soon as I get a bearing as to where I am."

I smile at him to say "I need to know. I appreciate your patience."

He points down the street in the direction he has come. "Vidya Books. Left and right, a small shop, they have English." He looks at me, takes my arm so I cannot go. He gestures. He wants to take me. It is so easy for me, but he has turned around and is now retracing his steps. He does not want me to get lost. It is easier to show than to tell. He does not want me to think less of his city and its people.

In no time we are standing before a store. He points. "Here." But it is a restaurant. The sign is clear: "Veg & Non-Veg."

"In the back you will find."

He points again, now to a smaller sign at the corner of the window near the entrance door: "Vidya Books at rear."

I thank him. I enter the restaurant. It is noisy and it is hot. I am pointed towards a table. I shake my head, no. At the back there is an open doorway, no door, just hanging strings of coloured plastic beads. Together they create a Taj Mahal in blues and whites and reds. Flies cannot pass, only people. You expect a kitchen, but there is not. Instead there are shelves of books.

Had that man not been there, had I not asked, where would I be now? I part the beads and enter the bookshop.

There were many foreigners. Mostly men, but also women. They wear kurtas and saris, but they are not Indians. This room, like the restaurant, is crowded. But it is calm.

GRACE

I was confused.

I had become unstuck in time. As much as I am here now writing these words, I was then in a hundred places at once, unhinged, unstuck.

I was still that boy on the cricket field, eyes hidden in the crook of my arm, hand outstretched in the direction of a falling ball. Was I afraid it was the sun I would catch, a fire that would burn?

And still I was that young man gazing into the hazy, tropical ocean air, not seeing anything, only hoping to see.

And I was a man in a strangely familiar land of moss and totems, surrounded by a chorus of seagulls and ravens, their calls amplified by a fog low over a calm, calm ocean.

And I was in London, still fearful that my life had no meaning, drawn to an art created by the hand of a master two centuries before. There I stood on the same ground as Blake. I walked the same paths as Wordsworth. Like Tagore, like Shakespeare, I pondered the human spirit. But unlike them I was confused and afraid.

All those things were still happening, all at once, in a jumble. I am running for Neem. I am feeling the heat exhausting from the wreck of a train. I am silently watching a ship weigh anchor, leaving me behind. I am frozen in my tracks by an image in an office appointment book, a mere diary. It is as if all those things were still happening. All at once.

But then I remember the woman on the beach. What is it about that moment that makes it complete and self-contained? It is not the same as the others. It is a moment out of time. It holds a gift.

With two hands, it offers. That rain, that breezeless wind, a grace that is a breath through my life.

With ease, I befriend the young men in the bookshop. They invite me to join them. I feel they have something.

Unless I step, I will never know.

RECOGNITION

At first, they didn't recognize me. They thought I was one of them.

As I approached, there was a man somewhat older than the others, leafing through a book about the Ajanta Caves. He looked up at me. With a knowing look, mixed generously with both acceptance and welcome, he held the book in my direction.

"I've been there," he said. "I mean I've never been there, but the drawings in the caves look so familiar. So many things in India are like that, so familiar. Maybe another life or something. Or just like coming home."

He was Australian or maybe from New Zealand. I was unsure at first. Later it didn't matter.

"What I'm really looking for is The Ramayana. Have you seen it?"

It was nothing that he said – or that anyone else said or did – it was their attitude. The gentleness, the generosity, the genuineness contributed to a tone, a feeling, a simple aura of acceptance and welcome. There was no questioning judgement, no competition or suspicion. These were people who were normal. That is all I could think: "This is what normal is." Not a new normal, not a redefinition or refinement. This is what normal is suppose to feel like, I told myself. It is suppose to feel like love.

"What are you all doing here?" I asked. It was a simple question, but one imbued with meaning, a question I was afraid to put to words. I paused and hesitated. I delayed, but finally I forced the question out.

"Shopping" was the simple answer. "Need to get a few things. Tomorrow we leave and go down the coast. That will be nice, to get out of Bombay."

"I mean in India?" What I was asking, what my soul and inner being were asking was "What does my India offer for you? You are from America and Europe, from the West where there is everything. What do you come looking for here?"

"Inner peace." One of the younger boys spoke quickly, but with an assured confidence. His youth carried his words and lit the room with an optimism. "India is like our home," he said, "our spiritual home. Even before we get here there was that feeling. It's like the rest of the world has forgotten, but India remembers. She remembers where we came from. She is the caretaker, the guardian for so much. And it's not just in the caves and temples. It's in the people, the people in the villages mostly. There's a dharma, a respect, a love." He smiled and waved his arm. "It's all here." He didn't need to say any more.

The others seemed to agree with the boy. They didn't argue with his words or correct his forthright manner. They listened to him as if he was speaking the words from their own heart. Each, in turn, built on what the others had said. They did not tear down. They helped each articulate.

And not for a moment did their attention turn from me. As if they were invited guests in my home, visitors to my country, they stood before me and wanted to know.

They wanted me to tell them about India. They wanted to know about Krishna and Ram. They wanted me to speak of dharma and duty. They assumed I knew the truths of the *Bhagavad Gita*, that I might be a poet of the spirit.

That is how it felt. I had approached them with a desire to know what they had found on the road to truth, this Sat Marg, on which we are all travelling. Instead, I was elevated by their humility. In their desire to learn as well, I was honoured.

I lowered my head before these men, foreigners, travellers, seekers. I felt humbled. "I know nothing," I said. "I know nothing of this India, nothing of this spiritual plain, the truths of this land. I am a traveller like you. No more. I have been around the world once, clockwise with the breeze behind and I have returned a stranger, even to myself."

I looked at them each. Their faces were younger than their years on this Earth. There was a freshness and fullness of heart.

"If these are saints," I thought to myself, "I want to meet their teacher. Surely, they are mirrors reflecting something greater."

I looked to them each again. "I want to be like you," I said. "Show me."

MEDITATION

That night I met many more of these people – these saints, this new race. I was unsure what to call them. Their variety in age, in nationality, in demeanour or any other measurement reached wide across the human spectrum. This was the world. This was a meeting of humanity, a congress like no other. These were children at play together, delighted in the knowledge that they were and would always be children. Secure in the knowledge that their play was the source of their joy.

Among the crowd that evening, eating and singing together, were also many Indians – men and women, young children. They were hosts, but they were also brothers and sisters moving freely.

Among the older men was one I knew. I gravitated towards him. It was Patel. I looked at him more closely than I had at the chai shop. Somehow my eyes were more open, more alert to the subtleties. He was older, but deeply unchanged. The lightness of his smile and the touch of his weathered hand on my forearm was as gentle as always. It was the heaviness and fatigue that I had known in him years before that was now gone, evaporated. He was reborn, a child navigating in an old man's body. A curtain had dropped to reveal a truer self.

"Greetings," I said – or words to that end.

"Namaste." His hand touched his heart. He bowed to me deeply, both hands together. He was bowing to my spirit. He was happy I was there. That I could see.

Patel told me to sit and to be still. He told me to be pleasantly placed towards myself. I said I did not understand what that meant. He told me to forgive. I started. I tried. He said to forgive myself first.

He said my road had been long, but not unusual. Seeking had been my closest companion, but now the trip was over.

He asked me to close my eyes. He said, "Tell the thoughts to go away. Forgive them for bothering you at this moment. Tell them to wait. Tell them, 'Later, later.' Be kind, not troubled.

What happened next is difficult to explain. Words have not been made to describe the state of meditation. Language allows us to bite around the edges, to nibble and taste, but never to report the essence. Still I will try.

Like a dream, never reported while it happens. Like an uncaged song, sweet and alive, but flying high. Like the moment of artistic creation, bright and new, unsullied. Meditation is an open window. We sit at the sill. A vista is revealed. There is no judgement, no anticipation, no memory or regret.

In meditation we are without judgement. We sit alone, but there is no loneliness.

And so I sat in that stillness. I could hear everything around me. In the distance, the sound of the children playing was unchanged, but now I was in the company of their joy. A bird turned on the motion of a wing and I also soared. A scent as pure as a rose travelled in an unbroken line. I was there.

I am the smoke rising from the incense stick. I am the candle with a tall, steady flame. I am the ascent. I am that. And I am nothing.

There is no "I want, I need, I must do." There is only "I am."

And as that "I am" dissolves, it becomes only "am."

Then aum.

Then silence.

Do you know the feeling? Surely, you must have dreamt of this oneness, the knowledge that we are all together, not floating, not dreaming, not even doing or being.

I look around. Through my own eyes I see. Through my own ears I hear. Taste and touch and smell are one. These are my senses and yet they are only the tools I am given.

I rise above. The senses are for this world alone. I am more. I grow, yet I do not move. I feel everything. I want nothing.

This is surrender. Nothing is given up. Nothing is lost. I am still.

I am home, connected and complete.

BEACH

I am descending the path now, towards the beach. It has been a long time since I have seen this shore: the Arabian Sea gently touching my India. It is so simple here, a shoreline so unlike the rough rocks and driftwood and seaweed strewn high tides of Canada, so unlike the urban and industrial shores of city-harbours and ports, so unlike the chalk cliffs and shingle beaches of England. Another world this, but my world, even so much as I am now a stranger in my boyhood playgrounds.

I descend the slope, past the coconut sellers, shading themselves among the last trees and brush. The grasses give way to sand, the heat of the afternoon to the cooling breeze of the sea. I see before me a multitude of people, women and men both, Europeans, Americans, some Africans. It is like a new world, I think. It is a new world, I realize.

Descending the slope, I hasten my step. But I know I cannot go faster any more than I can go slower. The present moment has only one speed.

Voices are carried by the wind. Not so much voices or words, but laughter, an altogetherness, a unity. It is not the laughter that follows after a joke or the laughter of being entertained. It is the laughter of love. The laughter of brothers and sisters comfortable in each other's company. It is the laughter of children.

I am among the people now, spaced across the sands, moving. My feet are no longer hot, but cooled by the wet sands, the shallow warm-cool water, the ocean.

This is the one great ocean, the ocean that carried my puja coconut that day so long ago on Hecate Strait, the ocean that calmed when I did not know what was next. This is the ocean that carried the *Marathi Pride* from port to port, that supported our lives and our livelihood day in and day out. This is the one ocean on whose shoreline the children of the world play, the shore which the poet Tagore could see and, with his pen, did translate his vision to that strange English tongue as he rode her waves.

I approach what seems like the centre of that body of people. There is still laughter and calls. There is a running of feet on the wet sand, a playfulness. But there is also a soul-filling silence. It is a calm that is deep.

This is not a closed circle like a club or a nation, not like a church or a chosen number, select and few. This is one body. A humanity. I remember Blake's painting of Albion that so enamoured me at the Tate, feet touching the Earth, arms outstretched, welcoming and embracing in one gesture, humanity as one being.

I remember that day on Nargol beach so long ago and I feel to look to the sky, half expecting to see, to hear, to feel a rain that does not wet, but enlightens. I look instead at my own feet, always with me, carrying me across the globe, and now, as always, across these sands. There is no thought.

At this place, this centre of the world, I see a woman. She is seated on a chair, a chair so out of place on this wide beach, but yet not. Her feet, broad and strong, touch the lapping waters.

She is shaded by an umbrella. There is a coolness in the air, a surrender.

I approach and I am greeted by a smile, a welcoming wave, words in Hindi or maybe it is Marathi. I miss the meaning. I understand the love.

"From where have you come?" She asks. She speaks to me in English.

"Nargol. In Gujarat," I begin. I stop because I feel there is no need to explain my long journey. There are no words in me.

"Nargol," she says. "I have been there. So many years now."

"Yes. On the beach. I was a boy."

"You have come a long way." Her eyes are large. It is not disbelief or surprise. It is understanding. "It has taken a long time, but now you are here."

Love is something else that does not bow to the hands of a clock.

In that moment, I feel both innocent and protected. I am like a young boy. The moment continues. It does not stop. Like a note of music, sustained and undiminished, I am that boy on the beach in Nargol.

Then and now are the same. It is not a memory.

•

If you had this experience, you might want to run and tell the world. But after the running, the words will surely fail. In that moment, I want to run to Frieda, to find her and bring her to this spot, to this moment without a tick of time passing. I want to shout to Rusty, to Sharma and Sat. And Patel, certainly he is here already, among these people, so much at home.

Then I remember something that I long ago forgot – not forgotten, but secured away, wrapped and pocketed to be unwrapped now. Surprise and recognition in the same moment.

In a dream I was here. So many times.

I rise and turn and look across the sea, land and then water until it meets the sky, both without end. My eyes sharpen with a clarity.

I imagine a ship on the horizon. It travels north seeking a port. I see a boy on the deck seeking vision through a glass. I wave to him. It is a broad straight-arm wave of protection.

I beckon to him, join us. We are your shelter on these shores. Come home.

•

It is Ganapati's shore upon which the children gather. The dark clouds are distant and unseen. With shouts and dances, on that endless shore, the children meet. They are from all the nations. As one, they dance.

Somewhere a smile flits across the face of an infant. From where does it come? It is the innocent smile of knowledge.

REALIZATION

As I write these words, I am not the same. I am no longer just a boy dodging cricket balls or a sea-going valet, no longer a rain-soaked tour guide, a newlywed or a clerk knocking on doors. I am none of that. I am not. I have travelled the world, a circumnavigator by both chance and choice. I have ceased to be just an Indian. I am not a Canadian or an Englishman or a citizen of any land. I have found my roots. I have risen higher. That is how it feels: I am rooted, but I am stretching skyward.

When I say I am not an Indian, you may feel that I have forsaken my family and nation. You may feel that I am Westernized, materialistic, modern. No, I am none of those. It is something more.

I have not lived an unloved life. For that I am grateful. I am a part of all who I have met. My parents, like an archer, pointed me in the right direction. I stayed true to their aim. They released the arrow, but they are always with me.

So many friends I have met along the way. They are friends not because they were like me, but because they are different. We taught and learned together. They told me I was not alone. I tried to do the same for them.

Patel, Sharma, Rusty and now dear sweet Frieda each, in their turn, loved me. I learned of life from Sat, from Moses, from every person I met. Men like Derek stood briefly on the roadside, as much as to say, "Carry on. Don't give up." And from those I never met, like Rabindranath Tagore, that bridge between East and West, I learn truth and wisdom funnelled from the ages.

But I did not feel wholly loved until that moment on the beach. "You have come so far," she said. It felt as if the entire world could hear as she spoke to only me. "You have come so far." I could not remember any of my travels. My life collapsed into that moment.

A woman on the beach. She awoke in me a thirst when I was only a boy. She held up a mirror in which I saw myself and, as I looked deeper, I saw beyond.

We are each a reflection of God. But can the reflection look back and understand? She said yes. She said look and understand. You are loved. Without doubt.

•

There is a dance in this life, I was once told. Maybe it was Rusty who spoke those words sitting on a log on the edge of Hecate Strait. It could just as well have been Patel or even Sat. It doesn't matter. It is all the same voice now.

There is a dance, but we do not know the steps. We can barely hear the music. At first it is distant like a shenai beyond the horizon. It calls chaotic. A birth, a wedding, an end and a beginning. As we move and dance, we draw the melody with our steps. A toe points. A hand waves. We coax the music to the fore. We pretend to be a dancer. We dance until we think we understand. And then we go beyond.

What is this life of wonders? It is not for us to fully know. Does the flute know the tune? It is only an instrument in His Hands.

Put your lips, My Lord, together. Blow into this hollow reed. May the reed be filled by your breath. May the sound be pure. This I pray.

I am here.